SPECIAL MESSAGE TO READERS

This book is published under the auspices of

THE ULVERSCROFT FOUNDATION

(registered charity No. 264873 UK)

Established in 1972 to provide funds for research, diagnosis and treatment of eye diseases. Examples of contributions made are: —

A Children's Assessment Unit at Moorfield's Hospital, London.

•

Twin operating theatres at the Western Ophthalmic Hospital, London.

•

A Chair of Ophthalmology at the Royal Australian College of Ophthalmologists.

•

The Ulverscroft Children's Eye Unit at the Great Ormond Street Hospital For Sick Children, London.

You can help further the work of the Foundation by making a donation or leaving a legacy. Every contribution, no matter how small, is received with gratitude. Please write for details to:

THE ULVERSCROFT FOUNDATION,
The Green, Bradgate Road, Anstey,
Leicester LE7 7FU, England.
Telephone: (0116) 236 4325

In Australia write to:
THE ULVERSCROFT FOUNDATION,
c/o The Royal Australian and New Zealand
College of Ophthalmologists,
94-98 Chalmers Street, Surry Hills,
N.S.W. 2010, Australia

A CHANCE OF HAPPINESS

Never before had Petra felt such anger as that which she now directed towards the unseen Peregrine Arden. His mother was old, ill and uncared for — in Petra's eyes, his lack of responsibility was almost criminal. She just hoped she got the chance to tell this arrogant young man what she thought of him. But when that opportunity arose, she found herself flung into deep emotional waters — and in great danger of getting out of her depth . . .

Books by Diney Delancey
in the Linford Romance Library:

FOR LOVE OF OLIVER
AN OLD-FASHIONED LOVE
LOVE'S DAWNING
SILVERSTRAND
BRAVE HEART
THE SLOPES OF LOVE
THE SECRET OF SHEARWATER
KISS AND TELL

DINEY DELANCEY

A CHANCE OF HAPPINESS

Complete and Unabridged

LINFORD
Leicester

First published in Great Britain in 1985

First Linford Edition
published 2007

British Library CIP Data

Delancey, Diney
A chance of happiness.—Large print ed.—
Linford romance library
1. Love stories
2. Large type books
I. Title
823.9′14 [F]

ISBN 978–1–84617–943–3

Published by
F. A. Thorpe (Publishing)
Anstey, Leicestershire

Set by Words & Graphics Ltd.
Anstey, Leicestershire
Printed and bound in Great Britain by
T. J. International Ltd., Padstow, Cornwall

This book is printed on acid-free paper

1

Petra Hinton struggled along the windswept promenade, her briefcase in one hand, a carrier of shopping heavy in the other. The sea, angry and grey, exploded into white surf as it pounded the retaining wall only yards away from where she was walking. The sky was the colour of slate and scudding rain clouds came hurrying in from the sea.

Pausing only to change the shopping and the briefcase, each to the other hand, Petra lowered her head against the wind and the first flurries of rain and hastened on to her home in one of the narrow streets which ran at right angles to the promenade.

She had just bought a ground-floor flat in one of the grey flat-fronted houses that lined the road. It was small but it was comfortable and Petra, owning her own home for the very first time, was delighted with it.

As soon as she had turned off the promenade she was sheltered from the worst of the wind, but even so she was glad to reach the house. With relief she let herself in, closing the outer door behind her. Once inside, she set down her parcels in the hall and looked on the table to see if she had any post. There was nothing for her, but a letter for each of the other residents. Mr. Campbell lived on the first floor, and by rights his letter shouldn't have been there. He had a separate entrance up a flight of steps at the side of the house and his mail was usually delivered direct. Mrs. Arden lived in the basement, her front door opening off the hall next to Petra's own. She had not yet met Mrs. Arden, but understood she was an elderly lady who went out seldom, so Petra slipped the letter through the basement letter-box to save the old lady from having to come up for it.

As she opened her own front door

the telephone began to ring. Petra dumped her bags on the table and sinking into an armchair lifted the receiver. It was Tom.

'Petra? I missed you in the staff-room this afternoon, didn't you have tea?'

'Hello, Tom. No, I had some shopping to do, so I slipped away as soon as my lecture was finished. Did you want me for something special?'

Tom laughed. 'Of course! I always want you for something special! Actually, I wanted to suggest we went to see the new James Bond — are you doing anything this evening?'

Petra looked across at her bulging briefcase and sighed. 'I'm sorry, Tom, I really can't tonight. I've so much work to do, and with the end of term coming up I must break the back of it this weekend.'

Tom groaned. 'Not the whole weekend, Petra,' he complained. 'At least take tomorrow evening off, we don't have to go to the cinema if you don't want to, we could have a quiet drink, or a meal somewhere.'

Petra weakened. It did sound tempting. 'Phone me again tomorrow,' she said, 'and see how I'm getting on. You're probably right, I'll need a break.'

'Good,' said Tom with satisfaction in his voice, 'I will, and we can decide what we want to do then. Don't work too hard.'

Petra laughed ruefully. 'I'll try not to. See you tomorrow, I expect. Thanks for ringing, Tom.'

'I'll phone tomorrow.' Tom's voice softened. ''Bye, love.'

⋆ ⋆ ⋆

Petra replaced the receiver and sighed. If she was really honest with herself it wasn't only pressure of work to finish by Monday; it was also because she had moved into her own home so recently it still gave her immense pleasure simply to be in it.

She looked round at the little living-room, its windows looking out over the garden. There was a glass door leading on to a wrought iron balcony, for although Petra had the ground-floor flat, the ground fell away steeply from the back of the house so that it was the basement flat that was at garden level.

Darkness was crowding the windows now and Petra got up and drew her new curtains to shut out the early December night. Then she lit the gas fire, made herself a cup of coffee and a cheese sandwich and settled down at the table to tackle the work she had brought home.

As she sat reading and correcting her students' papers she looked younger than her twenty-eight years. For work she wore her long fair hair tied back loosely with a scarf at the nape of her neck. It kept it tidy without being severe; but as soon as she came in, she always released her hair, preferring it free. Unrestrained, it fell round her face in a golden cascade as she bent over her papers.

Her dark blue eyes, now concentrating on an essay from one of her students, were wide-set under delicate brows a shade darker than her hair, and her skin smooth and soft across her cheeks and forehead still carried the bloom of youth. Her mouth, now pursed in wry amusement at some of the conclusions offered by the student whose work she read, was full and inviting, ever quick to curve into a smile which lit her whole face. Only a firm chin gave a hint of another facet of her character, her determination and independence, and Petra was endowed with her full quota of both.

She worked steadily all evening, gradually reducing the pile of unread papers at her side. The history department of the Grayston-on-Sea Teacher Training College was not large, there were only two full-time lecturers, and as one of these, although her particular interests were archaeology and very early history, Petra was also required to take her students through to more modern periods. The end of her first term in the job found her conscientious and hardworking as ever, but extremely tired; a cumulative tiredness which had built up as the term progressed. Even as she worked she found herself nodding, and jerked awake realising she had not taken in a word of the essay she was reading. Wearily she pushed the pile away.

'It's no good,' she remarked aloud, 'I must go to bed. I'll have to finish these in the morning.' She left the work on the table and warm and comfortable after a hot bath, crept thankfully into bed to sleep the sleep of exhaustion.

* * *

Her slumbers were shattered by a pounding on her front door. For a moment the banging invaded her dreams and then she dragged herself from sleep as she realised she wasn't dreaming, but that someone was indeed hammering on her door.

In the darkness she groped for her clock and discovered from its luminous dial that it was twenty to four. Twenty to four! Who on earth could be knocking on her door at that time in the morning?

Still a little fuddled with sleep, she switched on the light, and stumbled from her bed. Reaching for her dressing-gown, she made her way to the door. Her father had insisted she put a chain on the front door when she first bought the flat and she was glad now she had followed his advice. Obviously there must be an emergency of some kind for someone to arrive at her door in the small hours of the morning, but even so Petra would have hesitated to answer the door without some precaution. She opened the door the extent the chain allowed.

'Who's there?' she demanded through the crack. 'What on earth do you want at this time of night?'

There was a faint light in the hall though the hall light itself was not on and in the half-light Petra tried to recognise her visitor. A quavering voice replied to her question.

'Could you get me a loaf of bread when you go out?'

For a moment Petra was speechless, then she closed the door a little and released the chain. Opening the door wider, she allowed the light from her own flat to fall on the visitor's face. An old woman stood on the threshold, dressed in a long nightgown, an overcoat and brown carpet slippers. Her hair, wispy and grey, stood round her head in an untidy halo, and her eyes, red-rimmed, peered out from a hollow-cheeked and wrinkled face.

'I beg your pardon?' Petra said incredulously.

'Could you get me a loaf of bread when you go out? Sliced.' She extended a scrawny hand.The fingers, left exposed by the grubby blue mittens were red and claw-like; and in them was clutched a pound note.

Still a little bemused, Petra took the

money. 'Do you know what the time is?' she asked a little less aggressively.

'Don't worry, dear,' replied the old lady, 'any time will do.' And so saying she turned away and moving unsteadily, went through the front door of the basement flat, closing it behind her.

Petra stared after her for a moment and then looked down at the crumpled pound note. Cold darkness crowded round the yellow wedge of light coming from her flat, and she shivered. She shut the door and crept back to the welcoming warmth of her bed.

⋆ ⋆ ⋆

In the morning Petra might have disbelieved the whole peculiar episode, imagined she had dreamt it all, if it hadn't been for the pound note lying on her bedside table. Intrigued now by this slight knowledge of her neighbour, she didn't sit down to her work immediately after breakfast as she had planned, but putting on her coat, slipped out.

The rain and wind of the previous night had died away leaving a crisp cold day, with the winter sun pale and yellow giving an illusory warmth.

Enjoying the sharpness of the air and the brave sunlight, Petra hurried down to the corner shop and bought a sliced loaf. She paid for it with the pound note and then carrying the bread and the change returned to the house and tapped on the front door of the basement flat.

Mrs. Arden took a long time to answer her knock and Petra was about to try again when she heard slow footsteps approaching. At last the door eased open and the old lady peered round it.

'Yes? What is it?' she asked. Her voice quavered. 'What do you want?'

'Good morning, Mrs. Arden,' said Petra cheerfully. 'I've brought your bread.'

'Bread? What bread's that?' The old lady peered at Petra even more suspiciously.

Petra held out the loaf. 'You asked me to buy you a sliced loaf,' she said patiently, 'and here it is. And your change.'

Mrs. Arden put out a hand to steady herself against the wall and Petra realised with a jolt that the old lady was standing on the top step of a flight of stairs leading down to her flat and that if she should lose her balance she would tumble all the way to the bottom.

'Shall I bring it down for you?' she asked, and taking Mrs. Arden's acceptance for granted added, 'You lead the way.'

The old lady nodded and using her stick and the banisters began her slow descent.

As Petra followed her down the stairs she was struck by the stuffiness of the air in the flat. The sour staleness enveloped her, making her want to retch and turn back to the door for some fresh clean air, but Mrs. Arden continued her slow progress and curiosity overcame Petra's revulsion.

The stairs ended in a living-room, cluttered with furniture and dusty ornaments. Petra paused on the threshold, horrified at the squalor which greeted her. Heavy curtains covered the windows and the room was lit by a naked bulb dangling from the ceiling. A table stood against one wall, covered with a dull red chenille cloth and on it was piled dirty crockery, plates of half-eaten food, the end of a loaf thick with green mould and a bottle of curdled milk. The chairs had clothes and rugs draped over them and enfolding it all like a smothering blanket was the smell, the sordid smell of poverty and neglect.

Mrs. Arden moved slowly to a high-backed armchair beside the table and sank into it. With difficulty she spread a tartan rug about her legs and then looked up at Petra.

'Did you bring the bread?' she demanded suddenly. 'Where's my change?'

'Here it is,' said Petra, forcing herself to enter the room. 'I'll put it on the table, shall I?' She cleared a space and put the loaf within the old lady's reach, and the change beside it.

'You could do with some fresh air in here,' she said brightly. 'It's a beautiful day today,' and moving across to the window she made to throw back the curtains.

'Don't do that!' cried Mrs. Arden imperatively. 'You'll let the cold in.'

Petra was about to say that it wasn't that cold outside today, when she saw that close to Mrs. Arden's feet was a small electric fire with one bar burning. It appeared to be the only heating in the room.

In time Petra realised that the malodorous atmosphere was not in fact cold, and that the warmth had been gradually built up with careful use of the tiny electric fire. Her hand fell from the curtain and she said feebly, 'But wouldn't you like some daylight? It's sunny outside, it'd be more cheerful.'

Mrs. Arden shook her head and

closed her eyes. For a moment Petra thought the old woman had fallen asleep and began to creep towards the stairs, but she was halted in her tracks when an imperious voice demanded, 'Did you bring the bread?'

'Yes, it's beside you,' Petra replied patiently and then on sudden impulse as she looked again at the revolting clutter on the table she said, 'Would you like me to wash those plates for you? It wouldn't take me long.'

'If you like.' Mrs. Arden seemed indifferent.

Quickly, so as not to allow her disgust to get the better of her, Petra gathered together the dirty china and carried it through to the kitchen. A similar mess greeted her there, and with a sigh she gave her attention to the sink. A small gas heater could provide hot water and amidst the mess she found an almost empty bottle of washing-up liquid.

* * *

It took three quarters of an hour to reduce the shambles in the kitchen to some sort of order, but at last Petra dried her hands and looked with satisfaction at the piles of clean crockery and cutlery on the kitchen table. Before she returned to the living-room, her curiosity overcame her and she peeped into the bedroom. It was immaculate. The bed, a dark heavy mahogany, was neatly made with a white lace coverlet, the curtains drawn back to let in the sun. Photographs stood in a frame by the bed and despite the cold of the room, the faintest fragrance of lavender lingered there.

Petra closed the bedroom door softly behind her. It was clear Mrs. Arden no longer used that room.

The old woman looked up as Petra returned. 'Where have you been?' she demanded.

'I've just cleared the kitchen for you,' replied Petra soothingly. 'All the clean things are on the table.' She paused, but Mrs. Arden said nothing, and so tentatively Petra went on, 'Haven't you anyone to help look after you? You shouldn't have to manage alone like this. Haven't you any family?'

'There's no one. No one left.' Mrs. Arden sounded tired. 'No one but Peregrine, and he doesn't come to see me any more. He's too busy, Peregrine is.'

'Who's Peregrine?' asked Petra.

'Peregrine?' Mrs. Arden looked up in surprise. 'How did you know about him? Peregrine is my son.'

'Your son?' Petra was incredulous. 'Your son, and he lets you live in conditions like these?'

'He's always busy, Peregrine,' remarked Mrs. Arden without apparent animosity. 'He hasn't time to visit me.'

Petra promised to do some more shopping, and then escaped upstairs to the fresh air and sweet-smelling sanctuary of her own flat.

She threw open the glass door and stepped out on to her balcony, gulping in the sweet pure air to clear her lungs of the lingering sourness of Mrs. Arden's flat. 'I'd like to get my hands on Peregrine Arden,' she thought viciously when she went back indoors and set about cleaning up her own kitchen. 'What kind of a man can he be to let his mother live in such a state!'

* * *

Petra spent the rest of the day working. She was determined to have as little of her work spill over into the Christmas vacation as possible, but when Tom rang she accepted his invitation to go out to dinner with pleasure.

Tom Davies was one of the natural science lecturers on the staff at the college, and as two of the youngest members of staff, he and Petra had gravitated together quite naturally. He had only been at the college a year when she arrived, but the sight of her, young, slim and very attractive, made him feel that the college had definitely taken a turn for the better.

On her side, Petra was glad to find the staff-room was not the retreat of doddering old fuddy-duddies as she feared it might be, but contained a staff of all ages, vigorous and enthusiastic, ready to help or advise. Of course some of the older staff looked a little askance at Petra's comparative youth and inexperience, but she soon earned their liking and respect with her competent hard work and happy disposition. She got on as easily with most of her colleagues as she did with most of her students, but Tom, with his curly blond hair and lazy grey eyes, was special and she enjoyed his company both in and out of college.

As she lay soaking in her bath, Petra wondered where they would eat. There were several quite good restaurants in the town, ready to cater for the influx of summer holiday makers, but she secretly hoped Tom would suggest Angelo's, a little Italian restaurant tucked away in an alley not far from the town centre, an intimate place where they could eat and dance. Suddenly she thought of Mrs. Arden and wondered what she was having for supper.

'Perhaps I should go down and see if she's all right,' thought Petra, and climbed reluctantly out of her bath. But she was already late and by the time she had dressed and made up she had only a moment to heat up some soup before Tom knocked at the door.

She let him in and accepted his kiss. He held her away from him, his eyes lighting with appreciation as he saw how her slender figure was enchanced by the simple dress of soft jersey that she wore.

'You look lovely,' he said and then added, 'Hey, where are you going?' as Petra pulled away from him and ran into the kitchen.

'The soup's boiling over,' she called back over her shoulder.

'Soup? I thought we were eating out. Angelo's perhaps.'

'Angelo's would be lovely,' agreed Petra, reappearing from the kitchen carrying a large mug of soup. 'This is for the old woman downstairs.'

'Downstairs?' Tom looked bewildered.

'I'll explain everything over dinner,' promised Petra. 'Just wait a minute while I deliver this.'

She went to Mrs. Arden's front door and knocked loudly. After several minutes she heard hesitant footsteps climbing the basement stairs and the door opened a crack.

'Mrs. Arden, it's me, Petra Hinton. I've brought you some soup.'

'Who?' The old woman's voice was sharp.

'From upstairs,' said Petra patiently. 'I thought you might like some hot soup.'

'Don't like soup.' The door began to close.

'Can't I bring it downstairs for you?' suggested Petra persuasively, putting out a hand to stop the door from closing completely.

'If you want to. I shan't eat it.' Mrs.

Arden had already turned away and was making her slow progress down the stairs.

* * *

Taking these ungracious remarks for assent, Petra carried the soup downstairs after her, with Tom, intrigued, close behind.

The sour air assailed their nostrils and unprepared for the sordid living-room, Tom gasped. Petra set the mug on the table, within easy reach of Mrs. Arden's chair. A dirty cup and a plate with some bread and butter on it showed that she had at least eaten some of the bread Petra had brought her that morning.

'I've put it where you can reach,' she said with a smile. 'I'll come for the mug tomorrow.'

Mrs. Arden remained unresponsive and Petra left, pushing Tom ahead of her.

'Heavens!' muttered Tom when they

had reached the hall once more and closed the door. 'I need a drink. What an appalling place.'

Over a delicious dinner at a quiet corner-table at Angelo's, Petra told Tom about Mrs. Arden.

'The trouble is,' she explained as she tackled a tournedo Rossini with enthusiasm, 'she seems to have no one to look after her. I mean, there's a son called Peregrine somewhere, but he doesn't seem to visit her — at least she says he doesn't and I can't imagine any son letting his mother live in such conditions if he knew about them, can you?'

'Perhaps he doesn't know,' suggested Tom. 'She seemed very odd to me. Perhaps she hasn't even got a son.'

'I thought I might try and contact him,' said Petra. 'He ought to know.'

'How do you intend doing that?' asked Tom.

'I don't know. Telephone book, perhaps. There can't be that many Peregrine Arden's, can there?'

'That's all right if he's local,' pointed out Tom, 'but I doubt if he is, or he'd know the situation.'

'The main post office has all the phone books,' said Petra.

'It'd take you ages,' objected Tom.

'Might be worth it though.'

'Far better to contact the social services and leave it to them. They might be able to find him, if he exists, and anyway they'd take over the day to day care of the old duck. They might even put her in a home.'

Petra looked dubious. 'I doubt if she'd like that,' she said.

'Well, go down to the welfare place on Monday and find out what they suggest.'

'I could, I suppose,' conceded Petra, 'but I think I'll give the post office a try as well.'

* * *

They finished their dinner in quiet harmony and when the music began again, Tom led her out on to the tiny dance floor and held her close against him as they danced. She relaxed into his arms feeling secure and content. She would have felt entirely happy but for that one worry that kept invading her thoughts.

It was after midnight when Tom drove Petra back to her flat. She glanced at the closed door of the basement flat.

'The trouble is,' she remarked, 'whenever I want to see if she's all right, she has to climb those stairs to let me in.'

'What?' Tom, with his mind on things far from the pitiful old woman downstairs, had been about to draw Petra into his arms once more, hoping she would ask him in.

He looked at her, uncomprehending for a moment, and she said, 'Mrs. Arden. She has to climb those stairs to let me in.'

'Isn't there a door to the outside down there?' he asked.

Petra shook her head. 'I don't think so. I didn't see one when I was down there this morning.'

'Well, there's nothing you can do about that,' said Tom. 'It's probably better if you don't go down at all. It's not your business after all. I don't see why you have to interfere.'

Petra stared at him, and suddenly thought how hard he looked, his eyes suddenly as unyielding as granite. 'People left old and alone like that are everybody's business,' she said, 'or should be. I'm going to make somebody do something about Mrs. Arden, and if you don't like it I'm sorry, but it won't alter my mind.'

Tom smiled. 'OK. OK. I'm sorry. You're quite right, love.' He pulled Petra into his arms and kissed her. She stood unresisting for a moment, then broke away, still annoyed by his attitude, and unlocked her door.

'Can't I come in for a coffee?' pleaded Tom when she turned back to bar his way.

'Not tonight, Tom,' she answered more gently. 'I'm very tired and I've still got a lot of work to get through by Monday. Thank you for a lovely evening.'

He stepped back, tight-lipped. 'I'll see you on Monday then. Don't work too hard,' and turning on his heel he walked away.

Petra closed her own door and sighed. She was sorry if Tom was cross with her, she was fond of him and very grateful for all the help and support he'd given her while she had been finding her feet at the college, but she hadn't liked the harsh look she had seen in his eyes when they had spoken of Mrs. Arden and she disliked being told what she should or should not do. Tom hadn't been dictatorial, but even so she took exception to his comments that she shouldn't interfere.

* * *

Tom didn't ring the next day and on Monday morning, the last Monday of term, when she met him in the staff-room during the mid-morning coffee break, he was still distinctly cool.

Petra, however, had had some news which thrilled her and ignoring Tom's cool 'Good morning, Petra,' and half-turned shoulder, she clutched his arm and thrust a letter in front of him.

Thawed a little by her obvious excitement, he read it. From an address in London, it graciously accepted Miss Hinton's invitation to come as one of the principal speakers at the weekend conference scheduled for the beginning of next term.

Tom glanced at the signature, but it meant nothing to him. 'Who's Nicholas Romilly?' he asked.

Petra's eyes shone. 'Only the most up and coming archaeologist of our time,' she cried.

'I've never heard of him,' said Tom.

Petra laughed. 'Well, you're a philistine, or the historical equivalent. He's written several books and has recently come back from Thessos, a Greek island where he's been leading a dig on a newly discovered site. I wrote to him care of his publisher — but I didn't think for a moment he'd come to a college as small as ours!'

Tom grinned at her. 'Well,' he said, 'it sounds as if you've landed a big fish. Does he give good lectures?'

'I don't know,' said Petra. 'I imagine so, but I've never seen him. Miss Danvers says he's marvellous. She's as thrilled as I am that he's coming. It should be the highlight of the conference.'

The conference, as it was always referred to, was a weekend of open lectures covering as wide a variety of speakers as the college could muster, offering an introduction to subjects which might otherwise have remained untouched, a chance to stimulate interest and further exploration.

Miss Danvers, the senior history lecturer, had agreed to find one of the speakers and after some discussion, Petra had prevailed upon her to let her,

Petra, write and invite Nicholas Romilly. His acceptance thrilled them both, particularly as he also said in his letter that he would be delighted to attend the reception held by the college Principal on the Saturday evening.

Tom was amused by her delight, and the constraint between them seemed to slip away. They drank their coffee together and casually he asked, 'Are you going to the welfare people?'

Petra looked up sharply, but seeing nothing but interest in his face answered, 'Yes, I thought I'd go at lunch time. I haven't an afternoon lecture today, just some tutorials after tea.'

'Would you like me to come with you?'

Petra was surprised. 'Haven't you got lectures?'

'I expect David would cover for me.'

'No, don't alter things. I'll be all right. I'm quite happy to go on my own.'

She did manage to get things moving

through her visit to the welfare office, and by the end of the week Mrs. Arden was living in a little more comfort than before. The circumstances were still far from ideal, the old woman insisted on keeping the curtains drawn so that she inhabited an artificially lit world where time played no part and had no meaning. Once again she disturbed Petra in the middle of the night with a request for bread, but the food problem had eased. Meals-on-wheels came each day and a health visitor would call regularly.

Petra herself visited Mrs. Arden each day when she got in, making her a pot of tea. Sometimes the old woman was pleased to see her, others she was remote, seeming not to recognise her. However, Petra did prevail upon Mrs. Arden to let her have a spare key so that she could drop in without dragging the old lady upstairs to open the door.

The social services had also agreed to try and discover the whereabouts of Mrs. Arden's son, Peregrine. For some reason, Petra felt this was her responsibility and visited the main post office to look in the phone books. There was no one listed under the name of Peregrine Arden, and the entries made under P. Arden were too numerous for her to contact every one. It was hopeless, and the last few days of term were too hectic to allow time for any further detective work.

'I'll discuss it with Mum and Dad when I go home for Christmas,' thought Petra. 'They might be able to suggest something. But I do wish we could find the elusive Peregrine Arden.'

2

Petra returned to Grayston-on-Sea early in the New Year, feeling rested and refreshed despite several late nights over the Christmas season. Her mother, delighted to have her home for a while, had spoiled her dreadfully, insisting that Petra sleep, uninterrupted, until she woke each day, a luxury she hadn't enjoyed for many months. She was able to relax in the comfortable familiarity of her childhood home and as the tension slipped away, her tiredness was drawn with it, leaving her renewed and looking forward to another exacting term at the college.

It was to prepare for this that she had come back early, for still being in her first year at the college she had no previous lecture notes to fall back on. Her work must be meticulously prepared so that she would never face the students unsure of dates or details. The broad scheme of the term was structured for her, but she had to flesh it out herself and be ready to lead her students on to research and interpretations of their own.

Besides the lecturing side of her work she also had teaching practice students to supervise for the first time, a prospect which she found a little alarming. It was a daunting responsibility to teach other people to teach.

On top of all this was the fast approaching conference weekend. Miss Danvers had told Petra that as she, Petra, had invited Nicholas Romilly to come and speak, she should be the one to introduce him before his lecture and, should he so wish it, accompany him to the reception in the evening.

Petra had been delighted at first, but as the weekend approached she found herself becoming more and more nervous. Suppose she made some elementary mistake, or said something stupid or ill-informed.

'Why should you?' her father had demanded when she had confided her fear to him. 'Keep your introduction simple and leave the hard work to him. Provided you've done your homework, you'll be all right.'

'Well, I have read several of his books,' said Petra, 'but his new one about his latest excavation hasn't come out yet. I don't think it's even finished. That's what'll make this lecture so special. No one will have heard it before.'

She arrived back at her flat in a taxi, for on her arrival at the station it was pouring with rain and she didn't relish the prospect of coming in to her unheated flat drenched to the skin. Even her dash from taxi to door left her damp and it was with relief that she picked up her mail, let herself into the flat and lit the gas fire.

Quickly shedding her wet coat, she dropped down on to the hearthrug and held her cold hands to the warmth of the fire.

When she was warmer, she leafed

through her post. There were not many letters but one, with only her name scrawled across it, delivered by hand, intrigued her.

Inside was a note from the health visitor with whom she had discussed Mrs. Arden's situation. It was brief and to the point and made Petra smile with grim satisfaction.

'*Dear Miss Hinton*,

We have located Mrs. Arden's son and he has agreed to a meeting to discuss his mother's case.

Yours sincerely,
Marion Carey.'

'So I should think,' said Petra aloud. 'It's time you took care of your responsibilities, Peregrine Arden.' Then she laughed, pleased with the outcome of her machinations, and decided that when she had unpacked, she would pop down and see Mrs. Arden, make her a cup of tea and discover if the son had been to see her yet.

* * *

Half-an-hour later she let herself into the basement flat. As she closed the door behind her she called out cheerfully, 'It's only me, Mrs. Arden. I've come to make you a cup of tea.'

Mrs. Arden didn't reply to her call, but then she seldom did and on entering the living-room, Petra wasn't surprised to see the old lady in her usual chair glaring at her. What she was not prepared for was the fact that Mrs. Arden was not alone.

Standing by the window, his hand on the curtain as if in the act of drawing it back, was a tall man, who at the sound of Petra's arrival turned his head and stared at her over his shoulder.

Petra paused in the doorway and then addressing herself to Mrs. Arden she said, 'I'm sorry, Mrs. Arden, I didn't realise you had a visitor.' She spoke sweetly enough, but her eyes glittered dangerously as she looked back at the man by the window. It must be Peregrine Arden.

'Oh, it's you at last,' said Mrs. Arden petulantly, as if Petra had come late for an appointment. 'Peregrine is here.'

'So I see,' said Petra coolly, and with deliberate disdain looked him over from head to foot as if viewing a strange and rare creature. He was tall, well over six foot, and his shoulders were broad in proportion. His hair, thick and almost black it was so dark, was cut short and swept back from his forehead accentuating the squareness of his face and the jutting determination of his jaw. Dark eyes, again almost black, stared out from beneath straight black brows and returned Petra's gaze levelly for a moment before he spoke, his tone clipped and haughty.

'Well. Have you seen enough?'

Petra felt all the anger she had known against him before surge back at the sight of him, standing disdainful and arrogant, superbly dressed in a well-tailored dark suit, immaculate white shirt and silk tie amidst the sordid squalor he countenanced as fit conditions for his mother. The contempt in Petra's voice as she replied matched that in her eyes.

'Quite enough, thank you. I was merely fascinated to see what sort of reptile you could be to allow your mother to exist in conditions such as these — ' she gestured to the filthy room with a sweep of her arm — 'when you are obviously a man of some means.'

'I beg your pardon,' said Peregrine with obvious restraint, 'but you know nothing of the situation.'

'Rubbish!' said Petra hotly. 'That suit you're wearing alone would pay for a home help for a year to keep this place clean!'

Peregrine raised no more than an eyebrow at Petra's rudeness but said, 'Possibly, but I hardly think that is your concern.'

'No, it isn't,' agreed Petra angrily, 'it's yours, or should be, but since you seem to have absolved yourself from all responsibility of your mother's welfare it has become mine, and that of anyone else with a modicum of humanity in him.'

Anger brought colour to Petra's cheeks and she found she was breathing heavily as if she had just run a race.

* * *

'Your concern — does you credit,' agreed Peregrine and though he spoke softly, Petra could see the fury burning in his eyes and recognised the tight control he was exercising on his temper. 'But it does not give you the right to pass judgment on things — or people — about which you are ill-informed. There are circumstances . . . '

'The only right I'm interested in,' interrupted Petra hotly, 'is the right of your mother to grow old with dignity, and the right she has to expect care from her son in her old age.'

She looked across at the forlorn old woman still seated in her chair apparently unaware of the furious argument surrounding her and then added, 'If I ever have a son I'll pray he doesn't lose all compassion as he grows up and become as arrogant, selfish and self-centred as you obviously are, Peregrine Arden.'

She turned on her heel and stumped back up the stairs, but not before she heard Peregrine's deep voice say, 'And let us also hope he develops better manners than his interfering and ill-spoken mother.'

Still fuming, Petra slammed her front door behind her and flung herself into her armchair. She relived the encounter and in her rage she found herself speaking aloud, venting her anger on him yet again with yet more instances of his negligence, the cold, the lack of proper food, the difficulty his mother had in moving about, let alone washing and dressing herself decently.

Gradually Petra grew calmer, but was still unsettled enough to find herself in need of company; the thought of an evening alone made her feel restless and on impulse she reached for the phone and dialled Tom's number.

'I'll be round in a quarter of an hour,' said Tom cheerfully when she asked him if he wanted to go out for a drink somewhere, and good as his word in less than fifteen minutes he stood smiling on her doorstep.

Seeing him standing there, so reassuring and kind, Petra felt a sudden rush of affection for him and gave him a hug. Not content with the hug, Tom lifted her chin and his lips found hers. For a moment she returned his kiss, then she broke away and said lightly, 'Happy New Year, Tom,' and stepped out into the hall.

As she pulled her front door closed behind them, she took his hand and said impulsively, 'Thank you for coming round so quickly, Tom. It is good to see you.'

Tom pulled her into his arms once more and kissed her again, this time more searchingly, his tongue flicking and probing, his arms holding her hard against him. And Petra, the tension and anger she had felt earlier draining away, allowed herself to respond, her arms sliding round Tom's neck, one hand clutching his hair.

Neither of them heard the door to the basement flat open and it wasn't until Peregrine Arden spoke that Petra was aware that he was standing in the doorway unable to come out because she and Tom blocked the way.

'Excuse me,' was all he said, but his voice jolted Petra like an electric shock. She pulled away from Tom and swung round to face Peregrine, her colour high, her eyes blazing.

Peregrine gave a mocking smile as he passed between them. 'Your loving heart embraces everyone, I see,' he said.

'Everyone except you,' returned Petra, but even as she said it she knew it sounded childish.

Tom stared at Peregrine's retreating back, and as the outer door closed with a click he said, 'Who on earth was that?'

'That,' answered Petra with heavy

sarcasm, 'was the famous Peregrine Arden.'

Tom was interested. 'Oh, so you found him then?'

'The social worker did. Much good will it do Mrs. Arden, he's about as warm and caring as a cobra!'

'You've obviously met before,' said Tom with a grin. 'Did it come to blows?'

'Not quite, but it could have if I'd stayed in the room with him any longer.'

'Well,' said Tom firmly, 'you can forget about him now. This evening we are going to have fun, so lose that bleak expression, kiss me again and we'll take the town by storm.'

Petra forced a smile to her lips, kissed Tom lightly on the cheek and headed towards the outer door.

They did enjoy their evening and she felt decidedly more cheerful when Tom returned her home later on. He kissed her again at the door, but anxious not to blunder on and kill off the new response he felt in her, Tom left her on the step and went home hopeful that at last he was perhaps making progress.

Petra closed the door behind him and sought the warm comfort of her bed. She too had felt the almost imperceptible change in their relationship and wasn't sure how she felt about it, but strangely enough as she nestled down in the warm darkness waiting for sleep, it wasn't Tom's soft grey eyes that troubled her mind, but the thunderous black ones of Peregrine Arden filled with contemptuous laughter.

* * *

Term started again and immediately Petra found herself involved in a myriad of college activities. Work immersed her, filling each day and overflowing into the next, so that she had little time for many thoughts which were not college-orientated.

She saw Tom most days in the staff-room, but their out of college contact was minimal. Supervising her teaching practice students took Petra out of college as well and involved her in late tutorials when the students had finished their day in the classroom. But Petra loved her work and thrived on the demands it made on her. She worked her students hard, but never as hard as she worked herself. Tom found it increasingly difficult to gain her attention; she had little spare time and not all of it was she prepared to devote to him.

Each day on her arrival home, Petra would visit Mrs. Arden, but she was always afraid of bumping into the old lady's son and so made a point of opening the door very softly and listening for voices before she ventured down the stairs.

Despite his apparent lack of interest, Peregrine did seem to have made some alterations to his mother's situation. One evening when Petra went down she found to her surprise that the stale smell was missing and a comfortable warmth filled the room in its stead. Surprised, she looked round and found that the room had been tidied, two electric radiators had been installed, and sitting proudly on the table beside Mrs. Arden's chair was a portable colour television.

The old woman looked up as Petra entered the room. 'I've got a television,' she announced waving at the screen chattering away beside her.

'So you have,' cried Petra, delighted. 'And radiators. Now you'll feel warm all the time.' She paused but as Mrs. Arden said nothing, her eyes once more glued to the television, Petra went on, 'Did Peregrine arrange all this for you?'

Mrs. Arden glanced at her again. 'Is there any tea?'

Petra smiled. 'Of course, I'll make you a cup.' She had got used to the old woman's non-sequiturs and abrupt changes of subject, and accepted that Mrs. Arden wasn't going to answer this question.

When she returned from the kitchen

she handed the tea to Mrs. Arden and said, 'Who cleaned round for you? They've made a good job of it.'

The old lady peered at Petra suspiciously. 'Who sent you?' she asked. 'You're not to open the windows.'

Petra promised she wouldn't touch the windows which were still closely curtained anyway and then realising Mrs. Arden was once more involved in her television programme, she slipped away.

Considering her visit later, she decided that if she were honest she didn't find Mrs. Arden a lovable creature, the only emotion she evoked in Petra, even after considerable acquaintance, was pity. But the old woman had not even managed to evoke that in her cold fish of a son. She might be a cantankerous old woman, but she was, after all, his mother and entitled, at least, to his compassion.

Petra still felt an extreme antipathy towards Peregrine, despite the improvements to the basement flat. These perhaps indicated that he hadn't realised the state in which his mother lived, but that in itself was no excuse. He should have known, Petra decided, because he should have visited her occasionally, even if they were only duty visits. It was clear he had had the place cleaned and aired and that he had made sure she should no longer feel the cold, but did he visit her any more often? Cheer her up with his presence? Petra hadn't seen him since the day she returned from her parents' and Mrs. Arden never mentioned him.

* * *

Life at college became so hectic with the approach of the conference weekend that, apart from a short visit each evening, Petra had little time to give thought to Mrs. Arden and her son. The conference programme had been arranged round Nicholas Romilly's lecture, as he was by far the most eminent speaker.

He had been invited to lunch in Hall on the Saturday, to deliver his lecture in the afternoon and to be guest of honour at the Principal's reception in the evening. A guest-room had been made available in the staff quarters so that he could stay the night afterwards if he wished.

He had declined the luncheon, saying he was unable to arrive before two o'clock but, as the lecture was scheduled for two-thirty, this would give him time to speak with David Hellman, the member of staff who had volunteered to man the slide projector, and to meet Miss Danvers and Miss Hinton, of course.

Petra spent the morning in a whirl of anticipation. She attended the morning session in the lecture theatre, an introduction to present day crafts, but very little of what she heard really penetrated her brain. She was going over and over her introductory speech and wondering what she should talk about when she met him beforehand in the staff-room. In the event, circumstances overtook her and her meeting with Nicholas Romilly was not in the least as she had expected.

It was ironic really, she had been sitting drinking her coffee by the staff-room window so that she should see him drive up and be ready to go out to welcome him, and then the Principal called her over to ask about the arrangements which had been made to bring Professor Romilly to the reception, and so Petra failed to see him arrive. It was only when Miss Danvers tapped her on the shoulder and said softly, 'Your guest is here, Petra,' that she turned and saw him.

For a moment she was transfixed with horror. She felt hot colour flood her cheeks and then drain away leaving her deathly white. Her dark eyes, large and luminous in her pale face, stared unbelieving at the man who stepped forward to meet her, towered over her, and extended a hand.

'Professor Romilly, this is Petra

Hinton, on the history staff,' Miss Danvers was saying apparently unaware of the confusion on Petra's face, or perhaps putting it down to shyness.

Professor Romilly gave a faint smile and said, 'How nice to meet you, Miss Hinton. To be properly introduced.' He was calm and assured, very much in control of the situation and entirely unembarrassed.

Petra forced herself to smile, but it was a poor effort. She took his outstretched hand and felt her own clasped for a moment in a strong grip. 'How do you do, Professor?' Her voice was faint and husky, indeed she had trouble in speaking at all.

'You're Petra's for today,' announced Miss Danvers cheerfully. 'She's introducing and chairing your lecture this afternoon and will bring you on to the Principal's reception this evening.' She turned to Petra. 'Don't forget to introduce Professor Romilly to David so he can explain how he wants the slides shown.'

'I won't,' promised Petra, and Miss Danvers went off to see how the lecture theatre was filling.

* * *

Petra looked up at the dark eyes regarding her solemnly from under their straight black brows. A suspicion of laughter lurked behind his gaze and in the awkward pause left by Miss Danvers' departure he said, 'Well, Miss Hinton, this is a surprise.'

Still rather dazed, Petra said as calmly as she could, 'Can I offer you a cup of coffee, Professor?' and then added a little more sharply, 'If it *is* Professor.'

'It is,' he replied blandly, seeming to enjoy her discomfiture. 'No, thank you. No coffee, but I should like to have a word with the man operating the projector, if you don't mind.'

'Of course.' Petra had taken a firm grip on herself and, apparently calm, took him across to where David

Hellman was waiting to meet him.

The two men held a brief conversation and Nicholas Romilly took a box of slides from his briefcase. While they were talking, Petra's thoughts were in a turmoil. How could it possibly be Nicholas Romilly who stood beside her? And if it was, and it did appear to be, how could she spend the afternoon with him, as his hostess, after the abuse she had thrown at him at their last meeting?

Her confused thoughts were interrupted by Tom who approached quietly and muttered in her ear, 'Is that your famous professor?'

Petra nodded.

'But he's — I mean — isn't he the son, Peregrine Arden?'

Petra nodded again miserably. Her day was ruined. All the happy anticipation which had buoyed her up for the past few days drained away leaving her feeling sick, depressed and empty.

'Has he recognised you?' whispered Tom, his eyes alight with amusement as he remembered Petra's account of her meeting with Peregrine.

'Of course he has,' snapped Petra. 'For goodness' sake, Tom, if you've nothing helpful to say, go away.'

At that moment Professor Romilly turned his attention back to Petra and noting her angry flush and the scowl she directed at Tom he said, 'How did you envisage the afternoon, Miss Hinton? Introduction, lecture and slides followed by questions?'

'Yes, Professor.' She cleared her throat and tried again. 'Yes, Professor, that would be just right.' And then seeing a hint of gentleness soften his gaze, she coloured again, furious as she realised he was sorry for her. He'd seen Tom's amusement at the ludicrous situation and he was sorry for her. To Petra this was the ultimate humiliation, and she knew her feelings were clearly demonstrated by the blush that painted her cheeks.

Anxious to do something, she looked at her watch. It was two twenty-five.

David Hellman, armed with the slides, disappeared to the lecture theatre and Tom followed him, to take his place in the staff seats. Silence slipped round them, the only two people in the staff-room and Petra said awkwardly, 'We're all looking forward to your lecture very much. I think you'll find the theatre's full.'

'Thank you,' he replied gravely. 'I'm looking forward to it, too. Time to go?'

Petra nodded and led the way through the college to the lecture theatre, packed with expectant students. They paused for a moment outside the door and the professor said softly, 'Wish me luck.'

Petra glanced up in surprise, but as there was no mockery in his dark eyes she smiled faintly and said, 'Good luck, Professor.'

* * *

They entered to a tumultuous round of applause and when it finally faded and Nicholas Romilly had taken his place at the lectern, Petra took a deep breath and stepped forward to introduce him.

She had taken immense care in her choice of clothes and before all her confidence had been crushed by the discovery that Nicholas Romilly and Peregrine Arden were somehow one and the same person, she had been pleased with how she looked. Her morale had been high as she regarded herself in the mirror at home. The cut of her skirt pleased her, flaring from the hip to fall in gentle fullness round her legs, her silk blouse, soft and creamy, had been bought specially for this occasion and made her feel chic and sophisticated. She had set out to make a good impression on the professor she had to entertain, and now that she realised all that was wasted effort, she was determined no one in the audience should feel her humiliation.

With a resolute lift of her chin, her confidence boosted a little by the faint rustle of her silk blouse and the swing of her skirt, she launched into her prepared introduction. There was complete silence as she spoke and when she half-turned to say 'and so ladies and gentlemen, I am proud and honoured to give you Professor Nicholas Romilly,' she was rewarded by a brief smile in acknowledgement of the build-up she had given him.

Nicholas Romilly's lecture was superb. He held his audience from the first moment, explaining clearly but without over-simplification how he worked and to what end.

He made use of slides throughout the lecture, to illustrate a point or an idea, and because of this he spoke in a darkened hall with only the reading light on the lectern to illuminate his mobile and expressive face. His voice, deep and musical, carried clearly through the hall, without apparent effort, and the light and shade of his tone kept his listeners attentive and interested. Everyone in the lecture theatre was captivated and when he came on to more detailed discussion of his most recent dig on one of the outlying Greek islands, Thessos, his own enthusiasm was reflected in the hall.

First he told them the legend attached to the island. 'There was a beautiful young princess, so the story goes, who was to marry a prince from a neighbouring city-state. But before the wedding took place he was carried off in a raid by some pirates. She sent sailors out to find him and to bring him back, but he was never found.

'Refusing to accept that he was lost to her and so marry another man her father had chosen, she ran away and sailed to the island of Thessos where she lived alone, waiting for him. While she waited for his return she had a palace built for him and a temple to Poseidon, the god of the sea. Her lover never did come back, but she lived there in readiness until she died.'

Nicholas Romilly paused and a smile lit his face. 'Those are the legendary origins of the settlement on Thessos.

Now I propose to discuss the more tangible evidence that we found.'

Tom had asked Petra if Professor Romilly could speak. Now he had his answer.

* * *

When at last he drew his talk to a close, he was greeted by thunderous applause. Students and staff alike rose to their feet. Petra too applauded, all antagonism towards the man temporarily displaced in her enthusiasm for what he had said. She had read several of his books, and had been impressed with their lucidity, but they lacked the direct impact of the man's personality. His own burning enthusiasm for his subject infected his audience and whether or not they had been interested in archaeology before, that interest was kindled now. And Petra was too generous not to pay him tribute.

Questions poured in from all over the floor of the theatre and with great patience he answered them clearly, trying to leave the questioner satisfied before moving on to the next question.

At last, Miss Danvers caught Petra's eye and was invited to propose a vote of thanks, after which Petra waited while the theatre emptied and Nicholas Romilly collected up the notes he had before him, but to which he had seldom referred, and the slides David Hellman had projected during the course of the lecture.

At last he turned to Petra and said, 'Well, that seemed to go all right. What happens next?'

'Back to the staff-room, I think, but you may find quite a crowd waiting for you on the way.'

He smiled, and his dark face was lit for a moment with pure mischief. 'It's nice to receive such a welcome.'

3

It took some time for them to regain the sanctuary of the staff-room. A large group of students, mostly those from Petra's own third year history group, were indeed waiting outside the lecture theatre and Nicholas Romilly was not the man to pass by and refuse to answer questions; but at last they closed the door and were left only to face the staff. Most of them however, after congratulating the professor on his lecture, drifted away, leaving Petra alone with her guest.

'What happens next?' he asked again as he accepted a cup of coffee and sat down in a chair by the fire.

'Well, nothing for an hour or so, then there's the Principal's reception. If you'd care to go to your room and rest until then, I'll come and collect you for that.'

'Rest?' The professor raised a quizzical eyebrow. 'Do I look that tired?'

'No, of course not,' said Petra hastily, some of her former antagonism returning; it was infuriating the way this man had the knack of twisting even the simplest words. 'I just thought you might want to change or something,' she added lamely. If not she would have to entertain him alone for nearly an hour and a half, and the thought appalled her.

As if she had spoken this thought he said, 'Well, you needn't worry about entertaining me, I'll be good and go to my room.'

It was said so innocently that Petra looked up sharply, trying to detect the mockery which must lie behind his words, but apart from a tell-tale twitch at one corner of his mouth, Nicholas Romilly remained serious-faced.

'I'll show you the way,' she said and led him up to one of the guest-rooms in the staff wing.

He paused at the door, turning back

to her and said, ‘Now you won’t forget me, will you?’

This sally drew an unwilling smile from Petra and Nicholas smiled too.

‘No,’ she replied. ‘I’ll be back between six and half past.’

* * *

By the time Petra returned to collect her guest she had been home and changed into a more sophisticated dress. The Principal’s reception was not a formal affair, but Petra had been warned by Miss Danvers that the women tended to dress up for the occasion.

As she had bathed and changed, the sole content of her thought was Nicholas Romilly. How did he equate with the arrogant, cold-hearted Peregrine Arden? There must be an explanation, for though the man was the same, his behaviour was entirely inconsistent. She wondered if he would mention Mrs. Arden and their previous encounter. He could have done so earlier, but apart from a veiled reference to it when they were introduced, he had made no move to explain or justify himself.

'He may be a brilliant lecturer and archaeologist,' she thought, 'but that doesn't mean he has no responsibilities as a son. Even if he's away for months at a time, *particularly* if he's away for months at a time, he should see that his mother is provided for and cared for.'

Petra had reached the same verdict as before, but this time she wasn't quite as confident that there could be no valid excuse; her judgment was tinged with uncertainty and it worried her. At the back of her mind were his words, 'You know nothing of the situation,' and though she had decided there was nothing she could know which would excuse the conditions in which Mrs. Arden lived, the words nagged her and she wondered if she had been quite fair. Still, she had to make the evening tolerable for both of them and she resolved that she wouldn't refer to Mrs.

Arden, if he didn't.

Wearing a clinging dress of midnight blue, scooped low at the neck hinting at what it concealed rather than revealing anything, and with her hair a golden sheen about her face, she knocked on Professor Romilly's door.

'Ready, Professor?' she enquired as he opened it to her.

'Yes, indeed.' He paused for a moment as his eyes swept over her with undisguised approval, and then said, 'Do you think, Miss Hinton, that as we're to spend the next hour or so together we could manage Christian names?'

Taken off guard, Petra said, 'Of course, if you like.'

'I do like,' said Nicholas and before she could move he leaned forward and, bending his head, kissed her on the cheek. 'Good evening, Petra.'

Her hand flew involuntarily to her cheek and she stepped back, needing a deep breath before she could reply, 'Good evening, Nicholas.'

'Better,' he said with a grin. 'Now, lead me into the lion's den.'

* * *

Nicholas mixed easily at the reception to which the fourth year students, the staff and other visiting speakers had been invited. He was charming and relaxed, talking easily with everyone, and Petra decided she could slip away once he was established and join Tom who was waving to her from across the room.

But as she moved from Nicholas' side, he put out a hand to stay her and asked her opinion on his answer to a particular question.

'Don't go off and leave me,' he murmured as Miss Danvers approached. 'You're supposed to be looking after me, remember?'

'You are perfectly well able to look after yourself,' snapped Petra, but she remained at his side while he listened with complete attention to Miss Danvers' congratulations on the success of his lecture.

'You've lit a fire of enthusiasm today,' she cried. 'Several of the students have been asking about joining the dig in the summer vacation.'

'If they can get themselves there, I'll be delighted to see them,' said Nicholas cheerfully, 'but don't let them think it's all treasure hunting. It's extremely hard work and at times back-breaking and boring.'

'Don't worry, Professor, it'll only be the dedicated ones who make the effort, but it would be a marvellous experience for them.'

'I agree entirely,' said Nicholas. 'There's nothing like practical field work to give insight into the whole subject. Don't you agree, Petra?'

Petra, whose attention was about to be claimed by the approaching Tom, turned back to the conversation and having had the question repeated, agreed.

'Have you ever been involved in a

dig, Petra?' Nicholas asked, refusing to let Tom detach her from him.

'Yes, in Northumberland. A Roman villa.'

Tom, realising he couldn't take Petra out of the circle of conversation, joined it, and Petra was forced to introduce him to Nicholas.

'I think we met once before briefly, didn't we?' Nicholas asked innocently as they shook hands.

'We weren't actually introduced,' said Tom coldly as he remembered the scene in the hall outside Petra's flat.

'No, of course not,' went on Nicholas smoothly. 'You were busy at the time, I recall.'

There was a glint of malicious amusement in his eyes as he saw the colour flood Petra's face, and she in turn glowered at him, furious that she had never been able to control her blushes whether induced by anger or embarrassment.

Tom, however, was not easily deterred and he said lightly, 'A group of us are planning to go out to dinner once this do is over. Petra's invited, of course. Perhaps you'd like to join us too, Professor?'

Nicholas smiled with regret. 'Thank you, no. I already have a table booked for dinner and Petra's very kindly consented to keep me company — after all Miss Danvers did say she was mine for today — ' and seeing Petra was opening her mouth to protest he went on smoothly, 'And we still have so much to discuss — haven't we, Petra?' His eyes, suddenly hard and dark as they had been when she had met him as Peregrine Arden challenged her, dared her to admit that he had not already asked her out to dinner.

For a long moment she was on the point of taking up the challenge and turning him down, but she was still intrigued by his dual identity and so she said to Tom, 'I'm sorry, Tom.'

Tom's eyes glittered angrily for a moment. He was as certain as he could be that no such arrangement had been made and he could feel Petra was drawn to this tall man who seemed able to dictate her actions all of a sudden; but he controlled his anger with the thought that he could see Petra every day and so was able to say, 'I'm sorry too, Petra. See you tomorrow. Don't forget my lecture at ten, will you?' He gave them a tight-lipped smile and returned to the group he had been with earlier.

⋆ ⋆ ⋆

Petra found she was clutching her handbag tightly, her knuckles clenched white round the handle. She felt angry with both men. Both of them assumed that they could command her attendance at the dinner-table without so much as a request, and she was on the point of turning back to Nicholas and saying she had changed her mind when he spoke again.

'Can we go soon? I really do want to talk to you in peace. We do have a mutual concern, remember?'

Petra sighed. 'Perhaps we should give it another ten minutes,' she said, 'then I think we could slip away.'

'Then let's have another drink before we leave,' and taking her arm, Nicholas piloted her across to the table where some of the students were dispensing drinks.

As he handed her a glass, Petra managed to free her arm from his grasp, yet even when he was no longer holding her, she seemed to feel the grip of his fingers on her flesh, a tingling patch on her skin.

'Now, where do you suggest we go to eat?' he said as they moved back into the crowd.

'I thought you'd booked a table?' said Petra raising her eyes to his in surprise.

'I'd got as far as thinking about it,' Nicholas conceded with a twinkle. 'But I must admit I was going to consult you on the subject as I don't know the town.'

Petra was at a loss for a moment, not quite knowing what to suggest.

'Where will your friends go, do you think?' asked Nicholas.

Petra shrugged. 'I don't know. Angelo's probably. They can dance there, too.'

'Then,' said Nicholas with decision, 'I suggest we choose somewhere else!'

* * *

When they emerged from the college buildings, they were almost swept off their feet by the gale howling in from the sea. It was bitterly cold and the wind knifed through them. Petra clutched her coat about her and her hair streamed into her face.

'This way,' said Nicholas and once more taking her arm, he hurried her across to the car park where his car was waiting. Once they were both safely inside, he glanced across at her in the darkness and said, 'That's some gale out there.' The car rocked violently as he spoke, shaken by a sudden gust of wind.

Petra said, 'It can blow up very

quickly in this part of the world. There are some nights when the windows rattle so hard I'm afraid they'll blow in.'

'Sounds as if you're in for a rattling night.' Nicholas smiled as he started the engine. 'Now, where do we go?'

Sincerely hoping she had guessed correctly about Tom's crowd choosing Angelo's, Petra directed him to another restaurant, Papillon, further along the coast road. As they drove along the promenade, windswept and deserted, they saw the pounding surf flung high above the road, sparklets gleaming in the light of the street lamps.

When they reached the restaurant they were given a quiet table in a corner.

It wasn't until they were eating their main course that Nicholas broached the subject of Mrs. Arden.

'I want to talk to you about — my mother.' There was an almost imperceptible pause before he said the last two words, and Petra looked across at him, wondering if she really wanted to hear his excuses, whatever they might be.

He put down his knife and fork and said quietly, 'Even a condemned man may speak in his own defence.'

The ever ready colour suffused Petra's cheeks. 'You aren't a condemned man,' she said testily.

'Aren't I?' Nicholas' dark eyes held hers for a long moment, seeming to search her soul. 'Haven't you already condemned me as a cold-hearted son who neglects his mother, when, whatever his feelings about her, he has the moral duty to see she is cared for?'

He had so neatly summed up exactly what Petra did think about him, that she found herself unable to return his steady look and lowered her gaze to the table.

'Will you listen?' He spoke softly and yet his question demanded an answer.

Petra looked up at him again and managed a faint smile. 'Of course,' she said.

'Good,' said Nicholas with satisfaction. 'In that case I'll tell you all about it over coffee. In the meantime, tell me about your Northumbrian dig. Was that the one led by Roger Garfield?'

Petra nodded and for the rest of the meal they talked, she realised much later, almost entirely about her. Nicholas was at his most charming, and Petra responded like a flower uncurling its petals to the sun.

⋆ ⋆ ⋆

When at last the coffee arrived, Nicholas sat back in his chair while Petra poured a cup for each of them, then without further preamble he told her about his mother.

'When she married my father it was her second marriage. Her first ended in divorce several years earlier, she'd been married very young after a whirlwind romance and I suppose they just grew out of each other, if you see what I mean.'

Petra nodded.

'Well, some considerable time later, I was born and on my mother's insistence was christened Peregrine Nicholas. In this, as in every other way, my father let her do as she wished. He was very fond of her and I suppose was afraid of losing her. He did all he could to make her happy, but it didn't work. She hadn't wanted a baby at her age in the first place and begrudged the time and effort necessary to look after a child. My father was a solicitor and worked very hard, often bringing work from the office to do at home. Gradually the rift between them widened, and when I was four, she walked out, ran off with a man called Jack Arden. I didn't see her again until the other day, the day you and I met in her flat.'

Petra stared at him, unable to speak and feeling sick inside. She had thought he was arrogant, when all the time it was her own sanctimonious arrogance which hadn't allowed him at least the benefit of the doubt, at least the chance of an explanation. In her own overbearing way she had marched in, passed judgment before she was in full possession of the facts and condemned Nicholas. How right he'd been to use that word.

Shame at her own behaviour overwhelmed her; she needed to apologise, to ask his forgiveness, but she didn't know where to start. But Nicholas hadn't finished.

'Some time later, my father divorced her and he too married again. My stepmother, whom I regard as my mother, gave me all the love, care and attention I had missed from my real mother. She and my father and I were a happy and loving family, as close as any other. My father died recently, but my stepmother and I are still as close as ever. You can imagine the shock when I was informed by a social worker that my natural mother was living in dreadful conditions in a basement in a seaside town. A strange coincidence, too, that I had recently accepted your invitation to speak in the same place.'

Nicholas paused again, looking across

the table where Petra sat pale-faced as if turned to marble, and for a moment there was silence. Then Petra buried her face in her hands, afraid the tears of mortification would overflow down her cheeks.

'Oh, Nicholas,' she whispered, 'I'm so sorry. Of all the arrogant, domineering, overbearing . . .'

'Who?' Nicholas interrupted with a grin. 'Me?'

'No, of course not.' Petra jerked her head up to face him once more. 'Me. Can you forgive me for all I said to you that time, all that abuse I hurled at your head?'

Nicholas reached across the table and took hold of both her hands. 'When you look at me out of those enormous blue eyes of yours,' he said simply, 'I can forgive you anything.'

Petra felt his grip tighten on her hands and smiled at him tremulously.

Nicholas smiled too and then said briskly, 'Now, let's have some more coffee, this lot is stone cold, and then

I'll tell you what I propose doing about Mrs. Arden.'

He ordered fresh coffee and then sat back watching Petra.

* * *

Still finding it difficult to come to terms with his story, Petra said, 'But why Peregrine? I mean why does she call you Peregrine?'

'I believe she always did — as I said, it was her choice of name. My father never liked it, and when she left us he began calling me Nicholas. I must say I'm quite relieved. Imagine having to answer to Peregrine for the whole of your life!'

'No wonder I couldn't find you in any of the phone books,' mused Petra. 'I was looking for a Peregrine Arden. How on earth did the social worker find you?'

'Quite simply, I believe. My mother, Mrs. Arden, knew the address. It was where she had lived herself when she was married to my father. I expect they caught her on a lucid day and she told them.'

The coffee arrived and Petra was glad to pour it out. It gave her something to do, but even as she did so she found her hands were shaking and the cups chattered on their saucers.

Nicholas appeared not to notice, for which she was grateful; she herself couldn't decide which had given her the shakes, her humiliation and subsequent apology or the strength of his hands and the level gaze in his eyes when Nicholas had accepted that apology.

'Anyway,' he continued, 'I've arranged for her to go into a home where she can be looked after properly. I know she thinks she can cope where she is, but she can't really.'

'And are you going to pay for all this?' Petra asked in amazement.

'Of course,' said Nicholas lightly. 'You aren't going to tell me I *shouldn't* be supporting my mother now, are you? There's no pleasing some people!'

'In the circumstances, I'd have said it was more than generous,' said Petra. 'You don't owe her anything.'

'She gave me my life,' pointed out Nicholas with a grin. 'It's had its ups and downs, but I'm grateful for it, you know.'

'Oh, be serious,' said Petra.

'I'm quite serious,' he replied gravely. 'I've discussed it all with my mother — my stepmother,' he corrected himself easily, 'and we both feel she should be cared for.'

'Does she know yet? About moving, I mean?' Petra wanted the subject turned back to the more practical side, away from the motives and reasons for Nicholas' actions. She recognised now that she was incompetent to comment upon those, and wished with all her heart she had refrained from doing so before. Nicholas might have forgiven her, but it would be a long time before she forgave herself.

'Yes, we've told her, though whether she's really taken it in I can't say. I'm coming down to move her on Saturday. We're lucky to have found a place so quickly.'

* * *

Nicholas settled the bill and once more they braved the elements outside. There had been no drop in the wind, if anything its strength had increased, and they were glad to reach the car.

As they drove along the promenade towards the road where Petra lived, the waves were actually breaking over the sea wall, driven by the fury of the gale. Spray engulfed the car more than once as the water was flung high above the wall and cascaded on to the road, draining back over the edge only to be gathered in by the next wave and pounded to pieces once more.

'It's a high tide,' remarked Nicholas as they turned into the comparative shelter of Petra's street.

'I've seen it breaking on the wall before, but never as badly as this,' Petra said. 'It's the wind that's driving it on.'

Nicholas went into the house with Petra and waited while she opened the door, then he took her hand and said with a smile, 'I'm glad you were mine for a while.'

Petra looked up at him silhouetted against the light, and said in a voice that was not her own, 'So am I, Nicholas.'

His fingers tightened their grip for a moment and Petra found herself being drawn inexorably into his arms, until she rested against him, her head on his chest and every line of her body pressed against his. For a moment they stood so, each sheltered in the arms of the other, he with his cheek against her hair and then he relaxed his hold.

She raised her face to look at him, and there was a moment when she thought he wasn't going to kiss her. Then his eyes darkened and his mouth came down on hers, his lips bruising and demanding as he crushed her against him once more. Petra clung to him, her head spinning, her lips parted to devour his kisses and to offer him her own. She had never known such passion in herself, she had never recognised such need in another, but finding both now she was carried away on a tide of desire which would have denied him nothing.

It was Nicholas who finally broke away, dragging his lips from hers and with the hands which had explored and caressed her willing body earlier, set her away from him.

'What a temptress you are, Petra,' he said with a twisted smile. 'But this is neither the time — ' he glanced round the hallway — 'nor the place.'

Petra leaned weakly against the door post and, as he spoke, suppressed a quick vision of herself in Tom's arms as Nicholas had seen her last time he was there. Perhaps he had had the same thought, she didn't know, but he didn't touch her again.

'Good night, Petra,' he said gently and turning abruptly crossed to the outside door. He opened it and the wind howled in, then he closed it again and turning back saw her still leaning shakily against the door jamb.

'I'm moving Mrs. Arden on Saturday,' he said. 'Will you have dinner with me afterwards?'

Petra nodded, still unable to speak and Nicholas smiled before he disappeared into the night.

4

Petra didn't sleep easily that night despite the strains and stresses of her day. The wind howled and moaned round the house, rattling the windows, a perpetual cacophony, but it was not the raging storm outside which kept her from sleep, it was the turmoil in her mind as she lived and re-lived the strange events of the day.

Each happening might have been enough to keep her awake, but all of them together made sleep impossible. She had run the whole gamut of her emotions, from fear and anger through to shame and love. She accepted this last emotion in its widest sense, recognising she had been tremendously attracted to Nicholas, his strength and his masculinity drawing her to him in a way no other man had.

She was, however, quite realistic

enough to accept that Nicholas had had no further thoughts than an evening together, the idea of it culminating in bed had not occurred to him and when it did present itself as a possibility, he had held back.

Petra was glad he had, though she still felt physically weak when she remembered the feel of his hands on her body, of his mouth against hers, because she didn't subscribe to the idea that for an evening to be enjoyable it had to end up in bed. It was one of the differences she had with Tom, and it was one where she was not prepared to give way lightly. But then Tom had never stirred her as Nicholas had tonight. Considering everything she was surprised Nicholas had kissed her at all. She was still stricken when she thought of the way she had behaved at their first meeting, and determined not to interfere in his life again. But she smiled as she recalled his invitation to dinner next week.

Turning over yet again, she thumped

her pillow and in doing so knocked her book off the bedside table. It splashed to the floor. For a moment Petra didn't register the sound then, puzzled, she reached out with her hand and felt on the floor beside her bed. It was wet. There was at least an inch of water.

Startled, she sat up with a cry and reached for the bedside lamp, but something stayed her hand. Electricity and water do not mix. Carefully, she pulled open the drawer of her bedside table and felt round inside for the little flashlight she always kept there. Taking it out, she quickly switched it on.

What she saw made her gasp with horror. She was marooned on her bed, entirely surrounded by water. Her bedroom door, which she always left ajar, now stood wide, pushed open by the pressure of the water.

* * *

How long she sat and stared in disbelief Petra didn't know, probably only a matter of minutes, though everything seemed so unreal it could have been longer. It was the sight of her slippers bobbing gently across the room which galvanised her into action. She reached for her dressing-gown, which lay across the foot of the bed, but quickly discarded it again, the end of it had trailed in the water and was soaked. Hitching her nightie up above her knees, Petra swung her legs over the side of the bed and stepped down on to the floor. The water which lapped her ankles was icy and she hastily drew her feet back on to the bed.

Think, she said to herself. Think carefully. Boots. A pair of Wellingtons she used for college field trips stood in her wardrobe and braving the cold water she paddled across and opened the wardrobe door. She grabbed the boots and collected a thick sweater from the shelf, and trousers from a hanger. Carrying them back to her island bed, she quickly put them on, feeling much less vulnerable than she had when clad only in her nightie. Dry in her boots, she left her bedroom to look at the rest of her flat. There was water everywhere, right up to her front door.

Petra was still confused. Where on earth had the water come from? Her hands were wet and unthinking she licked her fingers. They tasted of salt. Then at last she realised. It was the sea. Driven by the violence of the gale, the sea at high tide had breached the sea wall and flooded the surrounding streets.

Petra returned to her bedroom and looked out of the window which faced the street. Her eyes widened in disbelieving horror as, by the light of a distant street lamp, she saw a dark river of water swirling past, already well above the bottom of the outer front door.

She ran to the living-room windows and peered out. There was no light this side of the house and, using her torch, she probed the darkness of the garden.

She could actually see very little, but she could hear the water cascading relentlessly down the slope on which the house was built.

Then Petra had an idea. She dragged open the glazed door which led out on to her balcony and thus allowed the water in her flat an escape route. It gushed out spreading the length of the balcony and pouring over the edge in a cascade. Petra could hear it splashing into the river already sweeping through the garden outside the windows of the basement flat.

The basement flat! With a heart-stopping jolt, Petra remembered Mrs. Arden. Her flat could be completely flooded by now and Mrs. Arden drowned because she couldn't escape.

* * *

Petra's first instinct was to grab her key and rush down to the basement flat, but she made herself stop and consider. If she opened the door to the basement flat, the water from the hall would flow down the steps. Could she climb down from the balcony and approach Mrs. Arden from that direction? The climb was possible for there was a cast iron drainpipe running down the wall, but what would she do once she was down? She could never get Mrs. Arden up that way, and though the water seemed to be running down beyond the house, she had no idea how deep it was.

'And if I can't make Mrs. Arden open the windows,' thought Petra, 'I could well be stuck down there myself, for I'm sure that drainpipe climbing is not as easy as they make it look in films!'

There was no other way into the basement except for the bedroom window which looked out over a little area below the pavement, and this would already be under water, so Petra decided that she must risk opening Mrs. Arden's front door to try and get the old woman out.

Quickly she found the key and paddled out into the hall. The outer door was still holding most of the water out, but by the light of her torch she could see it pouring in under the door. Opening her balcony door had indeed helped to lower the level of the water, but it still swirled round Petra's feet as she shone the torch on the basement door.

She eased the door open and peered down into the unbroken darkness below her. The water from the hall rushed, gurgling, down the stairs.

Petra made her way cautiously down the stairs, calling to Mrs. Arden as she did so. The beam of her torch showed her that here the water was also several inches deep. She swung the light round the living-room and discovered the old woman asleep in her chair, her feet propped up on a stool, as yet above the encroaching waters.

Petra crossed the room and shook Mrs. Arden gently to waken her.

The old woman woke with a jolt and a frightened cry. 'Who's that? Why's it dark? I don't like the dark.'

'It's me, Petra, from upstairs. There's a power cut — ' at least I hope there is, thought Petra privately. 'Now, don't be frightened, Mrs. Arden,' she began but was interrupted by a loud wail.

'It's all wet.'

'Don't worry,' soothed Petra, 'I've come to take you upstairs. We'll get you dry up there.'

'What's happening? Put the light on, I can't see.' The old woman was completely confused and struggled away from Petra as she tried to help her to her feet.

Petra spoke to her firmly. 'Now, listen. The sea is coming in. Your flat is flooding and we must get you out. Come on, Mrs. Arden, we must try to get you upstairs.'

⋆ ⋆ ⋆

The old woman continued to ask questions, but she did allow Petra to take her arm and pull her to her feet. As her feet, still in their carpet slippers, plunged into the cold water she gave another wail of dismay, but Petra had been ready for her and keeping a tight grip on her arms, refused to let her sit down again.

'You've got to come with me,' she said desperately. 'Don't sit down again, please.' There were tears of frustration in her eyes as she hung on to the old lady. Petra's torch was the only light they had to guide them to the door, but at last, still protesting, Mrs. Arden allowed herself to be helped across the room, following its yellowing beam to the staircase.

Water continued to pour down this and the level was rising with alarming rapidity. Petra realised it must be coming into the flat in other places as well, perhaps the bedroom window had given in under the pressure of water outside. The thought frightened Petra and she tried to hurry Mrs. Arden's progress, but it was impossible, particularly as the old woman was still dressed in her voluminous nightgown, the bottom of which was now soaked and clinging to her unsteady legs.

Shining the torch ahead, Petra made Mrs. Arden go in front and came up the stairs close behind her in the hope of catching her if she fell. At length they reached the hallway and Petra could see to her relief that the front door was still holding.

She guided the old lady into her own flat and because the water was now flowing out more quickly than it was flowing in and the level had dropped, she managed to force her front door shut. But having the balcony door open had allowed the freezing air outside to invade the flat and the living-room, particularly, was extremely cold.

Petra closed that door now as the incoming flow was cut down by the front door, and then deciding that the bedroom would probably be a little warmer, led Mrs. Arden through and sat her down on the bed.

* * *

Once again Petra peered out of the window to find the water still surging by. All the houses were in darkness, but she was sure other anxious faces must be pressed to the windows waiting for the help which she was sure was on the way. As she looked across at the houses opposite, Petra saw that the water was not far below window level and realised it must be the same below her. She opened the window and leaning out shone the torch downwards, shuddering as she found the sea bubbling and sucking only a foot below her.

Quickly she closed the window again. 'We've got to get out of here,' thought Petra. 'We must get up to the next floor somehow.' But the only way up to the first floor was to climb out of a window. Since the house had been converted into self-contained flats, there was no longer an indoor staircase.

Quickly Petra darted to her balcony door. She stood on the balcony above the tumbling water and looked upward. There was a window above hers, but no means of reaching it. Even if she managed to alert Mr. Campbell, they would never get Mrs. Arden to safety that way.

She hurried back to the bedroom, sloshing through the water still lying on the floor.

As she crossed the living-room the beam of her torch picked out the telephone. 'Fool!' she cried aloud and snatched off the receiver. The line was dead. 'Damn.' She spoke softly and clearly. 'Damn, damn!'

Dropping the receiver back into its cradle, she went back to Mrs. Arden. She looked up suddenly as Petra came in and demanded, 'Where's Peregrine? Does he know the pipe's burst?'

The ludicrous suggestion that all the water around them could have come from a burst pipe made Petra laugh; then she said, 'I'm sure he'll come as soon as he can. Don't worry. I'm going to put a message out to the rescuers. Someone's sure to come soon. The police will be out in boats, I expect.'

* * *

Leaving Mrs. Arden in the dark for a moment, Petra hurriedly found a white pillowcase and a thick red felt pen which she normally used for diagrams and posters. Quickly she scrawled HELP S.O.S. on the pillowcase and returning to the bedroom, pushed up the sash and leant out. She had intended to hang the pillowcase from the sill, but realising now it might well float away she went back in, collected a couple of drawing-pins, and sitting on the sill reached up and pinned her distress signal to the top part of the frame.

Her torch beam was fading fast now and it wasn't until Mrs. Arden said with sudden lucidity, 'Haven't you got any candles?' that Petra remembered she had. She went to find them and soon she and the indomitable old lady were sitting in the bedroom in the flickering light given by two elegant red candles Petra had once bought for a dinner party.

She found a towel to dry Mrs. Arden, but the old woman had refused point-blank to remove her soaking clothes and in the end Petra had to settle for wrapping a blanket round her and hoping she wouldn't catch pneumonia. It was too cold to keep the window open, but Petra sat beside it scanning the street for any signs of a rescue party. There were flickering lights in several houses now as people awoke to discover their plight and managed to find flashlights and candles.

Suddenly, Petra realised the water level was rising again and went quickly through to open the balcony door. Once again the water gushed away and Petra thanked God she had such a safety valve.

Despite the cold she left that door open this time in the desperate hope that any more water seeping in would not get as far as the bedroom.

'Where's Peregrine?' demanded Mrs. Arden. 'You said he was coming.'

'I'm sure he will, as soon as he can,'

said Petra reassuringly. 'But the streets are under water too, you know. It won't be easy for him.'

* * *

How long she sat beside the window Petra did not know. The slow minutes crept away as she concentrated on the flooded world outside. At last she saw them, a small motor boat with a spotlight moving slowly along the water-filled street.

'Thank heaven!' Petra cried aloud. 'Here come the police.' She opened the window again and as they approached, listened with relief to the man in the bows of the boat who was speaking through a loud hailer.

'Please signal if you have anyone injured or infirm in the house. Signal to us if there is anyone injured or infirm in your house.'

Petra waved frantically and at last the boat drew level with the window.

'There's an old lady here,' she called.

'I've got her up from the basement flat, but she's soaking wet and cold and I've no light or heat.'

'Is your flat under water?' the man called as he saw how close the sea was to the window sill.

'Not completely, but we can't get out.'

'Hang on, and I'll radio a rescue boat. Stay by the window and have the old lady ready.'

The boat moved on, broadcasting its message and answering signals from other houses in the street, particularly those like Petra's which had been divided into flats.

Petra turned back inside to look at Mrs. Arden. How would they ever get her out through the window? She had trouble enough moving at the best of times, but to heave her out into a boat bobbing below her might prove well-nigh impossible. Still, she must get her ready; perhaps she should tie something round her just in case she did fall.

* * *

Quickly, Petra moved the old lady to the window, seating her on the chair there and then she pulled a sheet off her bed, twisted it into a makeshift rope and secured it round the old woman's middle.

Within a few minutes another boat arrived, a much bigger boat which already held two people huddled together, wrapped in blankets. Petra leant out of the window and called and the boat came over, manoeuvring carefully under the window-sill.

'Who have we got?' demanded one of the men, holding on to the window to keep the boat steady.

'Mrs. Arden, from the basement flat. She can't move at all easily and she's soaking wet and cold.'

'Can you sit on the window ledge, love?' the rescuer asked, turning to Mrs. Arden. But she gave no sign that she had heard him, merely continuing to stare vacantly ahead of her.

‘I’ll try and get her to do it,’ said Petra. ‘I’ve tied a sheet round her like a rope; just in case she slips.’

‘Well done,’ said the man. ‘We’ll manage. Hold steady, Charlie,’ he called to his assistant. ‘Now, if you can sit her on the sill, we’ll try and swing her legs round. I’ll hold her this side, you hold her that. Think you can?’

Petra nodded and helping Mrs. Arden to her feet, pushed her against the sill. It was no easy task, but at last they got her round and with Petra actually sitting on the window-sill beside her, managed to ease her into the boat.

What happened next, Petra never knew, but as Mrs. Arden’s weight went from her grasp, she herself slipped and fell sideways out of the window. The shock of the freezing water made her cry out, and she swallowed a mouthful of salt water. Coughing and spluttering, she struggled to the surface once again, but she crashed her head against the underside of the boat and remembered nothing more.

* * *

When she awoke, Petra found herself in bed, warm and dry with a splitting headache. She opened her eyes cautiously and shut them again in a hurry as the light pierced her head and set it hammering in protest. After a few moments she tried again and this time, despite the pain, she kept her eyes open and discovered she was in a hospital room.

Petra wondered for a moment how she came to be there and then the events of the night all came rushing back to her, the flood, the cold, Mrs. Arden and the boat. Shakily, she raised a hand to her head and found it bandaged.

She closed her eyes again and lay still, her mind drifting back. She wondered if Mrs. Arden was safe somewhere, but it was too much effort to think coherently and she dozed again.

Next time she woke she felt a little

better and when a nurse bustled in she was able to ask where she was.

'In the General, dear. Now do you fancy a little drink of something?'

'A drink of water would be nice,' Petra said.

The nurse helped her drink the water and then said, 'Now have another good sleep and if you're better this evening we can let your visitors in.'

Petra wanted to ask how long she had been there and who her visitors were, but suddenly it all seemed too much effort and so she simply closed her eyes and slept again.

To her surprise, her parents were her first visitors. 'How did you know where I was?' she asked.

'The college phoned us, of course,' said her mother. 'How do you feel now, darling?'

'My head aches a bit, otherwise I'm fine.'

Her mother nodded. 'Concussion, the doctor said, and a nasty cut on your forehead.'

Petra had seen the doctor herself just before visiting time and been assured she would be up and about again in a couple of days. Her cut had been stitched and he had promised the scar it left would be very small.

⋆ ⋆ ⋆

Tom came to visit her, too. He came into the side ward with an armful of flowers and a look of concern came into his grey eyes when he saw the bandage on her head.

'You're something of a heroine,' he said when he had kissed her gently and handed the flowers to a nurse.

Petra was puzzled. 'What do you mean?' she asked.

'Saving that old lady,' said Tom. 'You got her out of the basement just in time by the look of it. When the water went down and they investigated the damage down there, they found that the high water mark came almost to the ceiling. She'd undoubtedly have been drowned if she hadn't got out and there would have been little chance of that if she'd been left on her own.'

'Is she all right?' asked Petra anxiously. 'Where have they taken her?'

Tom shrugged. 'I don't know. The professor was dealing with all that. She came into the hospital at first, of course, but I don't know if she's moved on yet.'

'What about the flat?' Petra asked. 'My flat, I mean. Is everything ruined?'

Tom looked uneasy and said cautiously, 'Well, it is a bit of a mess, but nothing we can't put to rights. In fact,' he added, 'several of your students have already offered to form a working party, so it shouldn't be too long before you can move back in.'

'I'm coming out of here in a couple of days,' said Petra. 'I suppose I'll have to find somewhere to stay.' She sighed, feeling suddenly tired and depressed again.

'No problem,' said Tom more cheerfully as he felt the conversation move to safer ground. 'The Principal says you're to move into the college guest-room for the time being, just till you get straight.' Tom didn't want to say how long that might be. The state of Petra's flat had appalled him, and he could see she was still nothing like her resilient self.

Petra managed a weak smile. 'That's kind. Say thank you for me, will you, Tom?'

He got to his feet. 'You just have a good rest and get yourself better,' he said, and kissing her once more he turned and left the room.

* * *

Petra lay with her eyes closed, trying not to cry. Tears won't help, she told herself angrily. But the thought of her flat, the home she had made for herself, being ruined by the sea made it impossible not to weep. Her parents hadn't mentioned the condition of her flat, but recalling their suggestion that she come home for a few days to recover, made Petra realise that they must have been working up to tell her about it when they considered her well enough.

The side-ward door opened softly and thinking it might be Tom come back or the nurse, and not wanting to see either, Petra kept her eyes shut and pretended to be asleep. But whoever it was didn't creep out again when he saw her apparently asleep, he drew up a chair, sat down quietly at the bedside and reaching over drew Petra's hand into his own warm grasp.

At this she did open her eyes and found herself looking up into the dark eyes of Nicholas Romilly. He smiled at her and said softly, 'Hello.'

'Nicholas!'

'I'm glad you're awake. Last time I came you were out for the count.'

'You came before? I didn't know.'

'Well, I wanted to see you were all right before I went home; I wanted to thank you for rescuing — my mother. She owes her life to you, you know.

She'd never have got out on her own. The home help must have left the bedroom window open on Friday and the water simply poured in. All the other windows were tight shut as usual and the place simply filled up like a goldfish bowl.'

'Where is she now? Is she all right?'

'Yes, she's fine. They kept her in here for a couple of days and then yesterday I moved her into a nursing-home. When she's quite recovered from the shock she can go to the old people's home as I'd originally arranged.'

'What'll you do with her flat?' asked Petra, without admitting even to herself the importance of his answer.

'I'm not sure yet. It'll have to be cleaned and decorated from top to bottom before I can do anything with it. Everything is saturated and discoloured by the sea water and there is an overlay of mud almost everywhere.'

⋆ ⋆ ⋆

Petra's eyes closed for a moment and then she asked, 'Is mine as bad?'

Nicholas had retained her hand in his all the while they talked, but now he carried it to his cheek and, pressing it hard against him, said, 'Where the sea was, yes, I'm afraid it is. But the water didn't rise all that high. You'd opened your balcony door, hadn't you?'

Petra nodded wearily.

'Well, because you thought of doing that, you should be able to salvage a fair amount.'

He sat with her hand to his face for a moment or two, and then turning it over, placed a kiss in its palm. 'I'm going now,' he said. 'I was told not to tire you, and you look worn out.' He got up and gently tucked her hand back under the covers.

'I shan't be down on Saturday after all. Mrs. Arden'll stay in the nursing-home for a week or so, but I hope to move her the next Saturday. Shall we make our dinner date for then? You should feel more like it yourself then, too, I expect.'

Petra smiled. 'That'll be lovely,' she said, feeling happier than she had since the night of the flood. 'I'll be staying at the college until the flat is habitable again.'

'I'll ring you there.' And with a featherlight touch of his hand he was gone.

5

Tom collected Petra from the hospital and drove her to the college. Although the doctor had agreed she could be discharged, he had warned her to take things easy for several more days. But once clear of the hospital, Petra felt her spirits lift, and felt ready to return to her normal life.

As they drove through the town, she stared in fascinated horror at the damage caused by the floods. The promenade was cordoned off in places where the sea wall had completely collapsed, and work was already in train to rebuild the breaches now only hastily repaired with sandbags. There were uprooted trees and shrubs in the ornamental gardens, so popular with summer visitors, and there were still layers of stinking black mud on the grass in the park where the street cleaners were unable to clean. The sea had flooded one end of the town leaving behind it chaos and destruction. There was débris everywhere.

Petra wanted to visit her flat at once, but Tom refused to take her there yet.

'Tomorrow is soon enough for that,' he said firmly. 'Let's get you settled into your room in college first.'

'But I need clothes and some of my personal things,' Petra protested.

'I've brought some over already,' said Tom. 'There were plenty of clothes the sea hadn't touched. Now remember what the doctor said, 'Take it steady and you'll be fine.''

Petra found her room had been made ready for her and, having reached it, sank gratefully into a chair. Tom was right really, she'd be far better facing the mess in her flat tomorrow. She looked round the room, the room Nicholas had occupied the night after the lecture, the night of the flood. Today is Thursday, she thought, only five days since the conference. It feels like a million years.

She dragged her attention back to Tom, who was telling her what had been prepared.

'Sally Harmer made up the bed and unpacked for you,' he was saying. 'It's Sally, actually, who's organising the group of students who've volunteered to help get your flat straight.'

'That's kind of her, Tom. And kind of you, too, to organise it all for me. I don't know how I'd have managed on my own.'

Tom's gaze rested on her for a moment before he said, 'Well, we're all proud of you. But I will admit you gave us all a fright.'

'I'm fine now, though,' protested Petra, forcing a lighter note into her voice. Tom's intense stare made her uncomfortable. It was only recently he had begun to look at her in that way, and it was very much a departure from the casual, comfortable relationship they had had at first. And as this thought clung in her mind, so she withdrew from him and when he knelt beside her chair and took her in his arms she tried to pull away.

'Come on, Petra,' he coaxed. 'Just a little cuddle. I've been so worried about you.'

She let him kiss her and wished he would go away.

Feeling her unresponsive to his kisses, Tom let her go. 'I'm sorry,' he said. 'I should have realised you wouldn't be feeling like anything much.' He gave her a grin. 'You'll be fine if you take things easy.'

Petra grasped at the excuse he'd handed her and managing a smile, said, 'I'm sorry, too, Tom. It's sort of delayed shock, I expect, but I do feel a bit feeble still.'

Having made certain she had everything she wanted, he left her sitting in front of the electric fire. 'Have a good night's sleep,' he said, 'and I'll take you to the flat tomorrow. I've no lectures in the afternoon, so we can go then.'

* * *

Petra had another visitor later that evening. The Principal came in to see if she was settled and to have a chat.

'You can have the room as long as you need it,' he told her, 'so don't run yourself into the ground trying to move back into your flat. And no college work till Monday at the earliest. We don't want any relapses because you rushed back straight away.'

Petra thanked him, grateful for his concern. She was relieved too that she need not resume work at once. She had wanted to, but even the short journey from the hospital had tired her, and she realised the doctor had been right after all.

Next day, after lunch, Tom drove her to her flat. The narrow street where she lived had been cleaned down but there were still plenty of reminders of the violence of the sea. Seaweed still hung forlornly from bushes, gates hung crooked on their hinges and the bollard at the end of the road lay smashed where a parked car had been swept into it.

They drew up outside the house and Petra looked down at the basement window through which the sea had poured unhindered into Mrs. Arden's flat. There was mud and seaweed still lying in the little area below.

She walked up the shallow steps to the front door. These had been hosed down and looking at them Petra realised that the damage would have been far worse on the ground floor if in fact the door had been at road level.

They went inside and as Petra fumbled with the key Tom said, 'It really isn't as bad as it looks at first.'

Petra thought she had been prepared for the worst, but even so she was very shaken by what she found. It was the smell that hit her first, the foul and unrelenting smell of the mud that the sea had left behind. The windows were open and yet the pungent odour had dispersed little. The dank air hung heavy about them, chilling and penetrating so that Petra found herself shivering.

Slowly and deliberately, she walked from room to room surveying the damage, trying to take in what needed to be done. The rugs on the floors and the fitted carpet she had put in the bedroom were utterly beyond redemption. The furniture was in varying states, depending on how much had stood immersed in salt water. The soft furnishings were saturated. The water had swirled round the hems of her long curtains and been soaked up so that the damp still hung at the windows and the material was stained and spoilt.

'The electricity is still off, I'm afraid,' said Tom, 'but the gas fire should work if you're cold.'

'Not that sort of cold really,' said Petra miserably. 'Oh, Tom, it's not fair.'

He put his arm round her and this time, glad of his warmth and support, Petra didn't draw away.

'Right,' said Tom briskly after a moment. 'Let's get sorted out. We must make lists of everything damaged for your insurance and decide what you are going to try and save.'

They toured the flat again, taking notes this time, opening drawers and cupboards to discover more evil-smelling mud inside and, in some cases, trapped water which cascaded on to the floor.

* * *

At last they had done all they could for the first visit and Petra had had enough.

'Come on, let's find a cup of tea somewhere,' said Tom taking her arm and propelling her to the door.

'Tom, wait, I just want to look downstairs.'

Tom stared at her. 'Downstairs? Whatever for?'

'I — I don't know, really, I just do. Morbid curiosity, I suppose.' She still had the key and opening the door of the basement flat, they both went down the stairs.

It gave her a shock when she saw it, for it was quite empty, not a stick of furniture remained. The curtains and pieces of carpet had gone and the windows, smeared with filth, looked forlornly across the ruined garden beyond.

The air was dank and musty, and the walls were streaked with mud almost to the ceiling. The place had been cleared but not cleaned. Petra wondered yet again what Nicholas would do with the flat now.

'Seen enough?' asked Tom impatiently as she stood staring, realising how easily Mrs. Arden might have died in the disaster.

She turned and gave him a bleak smile. 'Yes,' she sighed, 'let's go.'

Led by Sally Harmer, a large group of students set to work on Petra's flat that weekend, and when she next went to see it she found that all the irreparably damaged things had gone, the walls and paintwork had been scrubbed down and the gas fires burned full blast in both bedroom and living-room to help dry out the place.

Furniture they hoped to be able to repair or restore stood forlornly awaiting attention when it had dried out.

Petra joined them in their work and by the end of Sunday the contents of the cupboards had either been discarded or washed and stored in boxes until the cupboards themselves were once more in a fit state to be used.

Petra's parents phoned her often to hear how things were progressing, but although they asked her to come home yet again, she refused. She planned to start work again on Monday.

'I'm feeling fine,' she assured her mother, 'and I can't rely on other members of staff covering for me any longer.'

'Well, your father says you're to go ahead and order your replacement carpet and curtains and things. If the insurance hasn't come through in time, he'll advance you the money and you can pay him back when it does.'

Petra was very touched by this offer and thanked them with tears in her eyes. It meant she would be able to return to her home that much sooner.

She had been back at work several days when she found a message in her pigeon-hole. Professor Romilly had rung and would collect her at eight p.m. on Saturday. She read the note several times and found her heart beating with sudden excitement.

'Pull yourself together,' she admonished. 'You're behaving like a schoolgirl,' but even so she was still smiling broadly when she went into the staff-room for a cup of coffee.

Tom saw her and came over. 'You're looking more cheerful,' he said. 'Good news?' His eyes flickered to the piece of paper Petra still clutched in her hand.

Hastily, she stuffed it into her jacket pocket and said, 'Oh, just a phone message. Have you had coffee yet?'

* * *

Petra spent most of Saturday at her flat; she and her willing students had begun decorating and they spent a convivial day slapping paint on the walls and ceilings. With so many helpers the whole place looked completely different by five o'clock, clean new paint everywhere and the last traces of damp and staleness vanquished by fresh air and continuous warmth.

Petra stood in the middle of the living-room and announced, 'I shall be in the 'Admiral' tomorrow at lunch time and look forward to standing you all a drink.' This vas greeted with cheers and then the students disappeared to their normal Saturday evening pursuits.

Petra waited until the last of them had called goodbye and then wandered slowly from room to room. Thanks to their efforts and energy she might well be able to move back in next weekend. A glance at her watch told her it was time to go and she closed up the flat and hurried back to college.

In the front hall she met Tom.

'There you are,' he cried. 'I've been looking for you.'

'Sorry,' said Petra, 'I've been at the flat, painting.'

'So I see.' Tom laughed. 'You've got a smudge on your nose.' He raised a finger and wiped the paint away. 'After all that work you could do with a drink,' he said. 'Pick you up about eight?'

'I'm sorry, Tom. I'm afraid I can't tonight.' Petra felt awkward. Her dinner with Nicholas was not a secret and yet she didn't want to have to tell Tom about it.

'You're already going out, you mean.'

Petra nodded.

'See you on Monday, then,' and turning on his heel, Tom stalked away.

Petra stared after him for a moment and then ran lightly upstairs to prepare for her evening with Nicholas.

* * *

Petra waited in the staff-room where she could see Nicholas drive up to the front door. This time she didn't miss his arrival and went out to meet him. She paused on the top of the marble steps which led up to the front door, standing in the pool of light cast by the outside lamps. Unconsciously beautiful, her fair hair falling free to her shoulders, she waited for him to come up the steps to greet her, and when he did, mounting the stairs two at a time, she held out her hands in spontaneous greeting.

He grasped them in his and looking down into her face said simply, 'Hello, angel.'

She laughed at that and Nicholas said, 'Well, it's all that fair hair, all you need is a halo and a white dress and you'd be perfect.'

'The white dress is underneath,' she told him, still laughing. 'The halo I haven't earned yet.' Then feeling they were in far too public a spot with so many students' windows overlooking them, she said, 'Let's go. I'm aware of being the cabaret!'

Nicholas took her arm and led her to the car. As they drove to the gate he said, 'Right, which way to Angelo's?'

'Angelo's? Is that where we're going?'

'Well, you said it was good, so I booked a table, but I haven't a clue where it is.'

Petra directed him and they parked outside. Before they got out of the car, Nicholas leaned over and kissed her gently on the lips.

'It's good to see you again,' he said softly and then got out of the car and came round to open her door.

Petra found herself shaking at the touch of his lips and the closeness of his face to hers. Her heart was suddenly thudding and she had a suspicion that her legs might not hold up under her. As he walked round the car she took several deep breaths to steady herself before he should touch her again.

Angelo's was busy, but their reserved table was waiting in an alcove just off the dance floor. Nicholas ordered drinks and once the meal had been ordered, Petra sat back while Nicholas looked at her speculatively, his dark eyes taking in the silk dress, white as she had promised, which clung alluringly to her slim figure, and the softness of her hair against her pale cheek, the light dancing in her velvet blue eyes.

'Are you quite better?' he asked. 'No lingering effects?'

Petra shook her head. 'No, I'm fine, except for the scar, of course.' She lifted a lock of her hair away from her forehead where it had concealed the angry red line left by the gash. 'They say it'll fade quite a lot, and I can always keep my hair over it if I want to.'

Nicholas leant forward to inspect the scar, and unable to look into his eyes at such close quarters with any equanimity, Petra kept her eyes averted and her head turned as if presenting the place for easier inspection. She thought he might be sympathetic, but all he said was, 'It's been neatly stitched, it'll probably fade away to nothing in the end.'

'How's your — Mrs. Arden?'

'How's your flat coming . . . ?'

They spoke together to break the ensuing silence and then both laughed. The tension that had been between them broke and they each answered the question the other had asked, after which the conversation flowed with the ease of talk between old friends.

⋆ ⋆ ⋆

When they had eaten their main course, they got up to dance. The music was playing softly, not intrusive but persuasively rhythmic, and as they stepped out on to the floor, Petra moved naturally into Nicholas' arms. He held her lightly, delicately, as if he feared to hurt her, his arms gently round her waist and her hands on his shoulders the only contact; but as the music continued he gradually drew her closer until her head rested on his shoulder and her hands locked tight behind his neck. Still the music played and still they danced, their bodies moving in perfect accord. Petra's eyes were closed as she felt the strength of the arms which enfolded her and she thought, I could dance with him for ever.

When the music stopped they stood together for a moment before Nicholas released her and led her back to the table. Tucked away as they were in their alcove, they were aware only of each other. They finished their meal and relaxed over coffee and brandy, ignoring the rowdy group at a large round table in the corner, the other couples dancing, and those who sat nearby, hands clasped, heads close in intimate talk.

The band struck up a faster number and Nicholas suggested they dance again. He was an energetic and original dancer and by the time the music changed to a slower tempo, Petra felt exhausted and was helpless with laughter.

Nicholas caught her to him as before, holding her tightly, his face pressed into her hair. After a while she moved her face away from his shoulder and looking up at him said teasingly, 'You're not at all like a professor.'

Nicholas smiled down at her. 'What is a professor like?' he asked.

'Oh, I don't know. Elderly, staid, learned.'

'Whereas I am young, entertaining and thick.'

Petra laughed. 'Precisely! You're a fraud.'

'And you've found me out. Well, I'd better give up and come quietly.' The look that accompanied these words was a strange mixture of amusement and tenderness and finding it directed at her, Petra felt warmth stealing up her neck and spreading across her cheeks and knew that she was blushing. She returned her head to Nicholas' shoulder. Perhaps he hadn't seen the rush of colour to her face. She hoped not.

But her hopes were short-lived for Nicholas said, 'You always look enchanting when you blush, angel. Don't hide your face,' which only succeeded in making her cheeks warmer and his shoulder more inviting.

They had returned to the table when

a shadow fell across them and Petra looked up to find Tom standing over her, glowering.

'Ah, Petra. There you are. Enjoying your evening, I trust.' His words were slurred and it was clear he had had too much to drink.

Petra answered coolly, 'Yes, thank you, Tom. I hope you are, too.'

'Me? Oh, yes, I am. Of course I am. I always enjoy seeing my girl in the arms of another man.'

Petra flushed with anger and said in icy tones, 'I am not 'your girl', Tom. I never have been and I never will be. I'm sorry if you thought differently.'

'I did indeed. I did indeed. And you led me to think it.'

'That's utter nonsense, Tom. You're drunk. Please go away and we'll talk again when you're sober.'

'We'll talk now,' he said belligerently.

'Oh do go away, Tom,' cried Petra in anguish.

He leaned down towards her and she shrank away from him, dismayed at the scene he was causing.

Nicholas rose to his feet and putting a hand on Tom's shoulder said, with cold contempt, 'I think it's time you rejoined your friends.'

Tom jerked away from him. 'Well, if it isn't dear Peregrine. How's your mother, Professor? Still dying of starvation and hypothermia in a basement?'

* * *

For a moment Petra thought Nicholas was going to knock Tom down, never had she seen such fury on a man's face. His dark eyes burned with it and his face which two minutes earlier had been laughing and handsome, became a mask of chilling contempt.

Even as she watched him, Petra knew if that fury were ever turned on her it would cause a mortal wound.

Without looking at her, Nicholas said softly, 'Collect your coat, Petra. We're leaving.'

With a final glance at Tom's rebellious expression and Nicholas' withering one, she hastened to the cloakroom and by the time she returned to the hall, Nicholas was waiting for her, having paid the bill, and Tom was nowhere to be seen.

No word passed between them as they went out to the car. The beautiful bubble that had been the evening had exploded with a plop and there was nothing left of it.

As they roared through the town, Nicholas driving fast, Petra could have wept. How could Tom behave like that? How could he? She clenched her fists, biting her lip to keep back the tears of rage and disappointment.

The town flew by and suddenly Petra realised that the last of the houses was receding and they were out on the coast road. By the faint light emanating from the dials on the dashboard, Petra could see Nicholas' hands gripping the wheel, strong hands with long fingers.

Suddenly the car slowed and pulled

off the road into a layby, intended as a viewing point for tourists. The engine died away and they sat in silence for a moment. Petra found she had been holding her breath and let it out now in a long sigh.

'Well,' said Nicholas at last.

'Well what?' Petra felt defensive.

'Why did he think you were his?'

'I don't know,' she said lamely. 'I've been out with him, that's all.' She turned to face Nicholas and found his eyes intent on her. 'I don't belong to him, or anyone else for that matter. No one. Do you understand? No one.'

'I see.' He released his seat belt with a snap and reaching over to the passenger seat, very deliberately slipped his hand behind Petra's head, drawing her face to his. For a moment his dark eyes scanned her face — as if he could read my soul, Petra thought as she found herself unable to turn away. Then slowly his mouth came down on hers and she had no room for coherent thought. He kissed Petra as he had once before, with an urgency and longing which awakened an equivalent response in her.

She clung to him despite the awkwardness of the car seats. Her body arched to his and his searching hands caressed her to quivering fever-pitch.

Then as suddenly as before, he broke away and returning to his own side of the car rested his head for a moment against the side window. Petra watched him, his face illuminated in the weird green light from the dashboard. It was as if he struggled within himself, his face tormented as by some inner devil. She said nothing. Her own heart was still pounding, her body pliant and weak with desire. She had never wanted a man as much as she wanted Nicholas. Never loved with body and soul in concert. So she watched his private battle and said nothing, waiting for him to speak.

The agonising silence lasted thirty seconds, one minute, two — and then at last Nicholas spoke.

'Let's finish our evening on a harmonious note,' he said lightly. 'Will you show me your flat?'

'If you'd like to see it,' she replied, trying not to show how disturbed his kisses had made her.

* * *

They drove back into town at a far from sedate speed and before long came to a halt in the street outside the flat. Without a word, Nicholas got out and opened her door for her.

'Tom's never done that,' Petra thought inconsequentially as Nicholas helped her out.

There was a light on in the first floor flat, but the house was silent and their feet sounded very loud on the stone steps.

'I feel as if I'm trespassing or something,' Petra whispered and then forcing herself to speak normally she said, 'Come in. It's not finished yet, but at least it's clean and dry again and doesn't stink of mud.'

Nicholas looked round him and then said, 'You've made a good job of it, you and your students.'

She showed him round and then said, 'Would you like some coffee? The kitchen's back in operation.'

'That would be lovely,' he said and when she returned from the kitchen she found he had lit the gas fire and was looking out of the uncurtained window.

'I'm sorry there aren't any curtains,' she said. 'The ones in here were long and soaked up the sea water.' She put the two mugs of coffee on the window-sill, standing beside him.

He turned to her with a groan. 'Oh, angel, don't stand so close, there's so much I must tell you before . . . ' His voice trailed off as he looked down into her expectant face.

'Before what?' she whispered, reaching up to slip her arms about his neck.

He made no answer, but his arms closed convulsively round her and his mouth found hers. Petra struggled a little to pull away from him and he released her at once, but she didn't move far. She smiled up at him and said, 'There are curtains in the bedroom.'

He gathered her into his arms once more and with the single word, 'Witch!' carried her through to the bedroom.

There was no carpet on the floor, but the bed — being an old-fashioned wooden one — had stood high above the sea water and remained virtually undamaged, and the curtains hung at the window from which Petra had made her escape.

Nicholas deposited her on the bed, jerked the curtains along their track, lit the gas fire and then turned back to her. His breathing became heavier, his loving more urgent and Petra, as aroused as he, pulled him down beside her, and cried out her love for him in the ecstasy of her fulfilment.

They fell asleep in each others arms and, as she drifted into blissful oblivion, Petra knew she had never been so happy before.

* * *

She awoke to find him standing over her, already dressed.

'I've got to go, angel. Do you want me to drop you back to college, or are you going to stay here?'

Petra uncurled like a waking kitten and reached her arms up to him.

He laughed and bent to kiss her. 'No more, angel. I've got to be in Yorkshire by mid-afternoon.'

'Yorkshire?'

'Remember, I told you I've a couple of lectures to do up there this week?'

Petra did remember and pulled a face.

'I'll be back on Saturday,' Nicholas promised. 'Where will I find you, here or at college?'

'Here,' said Petra definitely. 'I'll be here.'

'Are you going to stay here now?'

'Mmm. I think so. Don't want to shock the night porter in college.'

Nicholas pulled the bedclothes up

round her and, holding them firmly in place as if to avoid further temptation, kissed her once more.

'I'll phone if I can,' he said. 'But I'll be here on Saturday.'

Petra heard his car engine outside in the street and then the roar as he accelerated away, leaving a silence hanging in its place. She curled up again and dreaming of Nicholas beside her, drifted off into sleep once more.

6

Petra spent Sunday in a happy daze. She met her students for a lunchtime drink in the pub as arranged, and then returned to the flat to finish the gloss paintwork. She worked alone, completely content in her own company. The shadow Tom had cast over her the evening before had faded away in the sunshine of her love for Nicholas.

Her heart turned somersaults at the very thought of him and she found herself laughing out loud for sheer joy when she remembered how he'd held her, kissed her, loved her. He hadn't said he loved her, Petra could accept that it was too early for that, but that he wanted her she was in no doubt and having recognised and acknowledged her own feelings for him, she was determined to do all in her power to turn that wanting into loving, not merely with his body but his mind and soul as well.

Pausing in her glossing of a window frame she said, 'I'm going to make you love me, Professor Romilly, or die in the attempt.'

Petra decided to move back into the flat as soon as she could. She would contact the carpet warehouse first thing in the morning. They guaranteed fitting within forty-eight hours and thanks to her father's generosity, she could tell them to go ahead. She would make her curtains and collect the chair covers from the cleaners so that when Nicholas arrived next Saturday everything would be ready and she would be waiting for him in her own flat.

Petra didn't see Tom the next day. It wasn't that she avoided him particularly, but she visited her teaching practice students in the morning and had lectures and tutorials all afternoon. Her lunch hour she spent at the carpet warehouse arranging for the delivery and fitting of her new carpet and kitchen vinyl, and directly she had seen her last student, she hurried round to the flat to begin work on her curtains.

She half-hoped Nicholas would phone, but then remembering she hadn't given him her ex-directory number, she realised that unless he had taken it himself from the telephone, he wouldn't. Anyhow, she thought, he'll think I'm at college, not here.

Petra didn't see Tom the next day either, and wondered if *he* was avoiding *her*. She hoped not. Although she had been angry and embarrassed by his behaviour at Angelo's, she also knew he had been drinking and had said more than he ought as a consequence.

* * *

It was Wednesday lunchtime when she finally bumped into him. Literally, in fact, as she hurried along the corridor to the staffroom. The pile of folders she was carrying cascaded to the floor and they both bent down to retrieve them.

'Thanks, Tom.' She smiled at him. Tom murmured something but didn't return her smile. He walked beside her however and held open the staff-room door for her. She thanked him again and was moving away to put the files on the table when he caught her arm.

'Sorry about Saturday,' he mumbled awkwardly.

'Forget it,' said Petra lightly. 'I have.'

'Really?' He sounded anxious.

'Of course.'

She smiled at him and he said quickly, 'Have a drink with me later?'

'That would've been nice, Tom,' she replied, 'but I've got the carpet fitters coming this afternoon, so I've got to be at the flat, I'm afraid.'

Tom didn't accept defeat easily. 'I'll come round there then,' he said. 'I'd love to see it now it's all clean and painted.'

Petra sighed inwardly. She hadn't finished the curtains and she had masses of student work to assess before the weekend. Still, if it would make her peace with Tom it might be worth it. She could always work into the small hours if necessary. Petra felt she could cope with anything just now. She was riding the crest of a wave.

'All right,' she said. 'I'll be making curtains, so why don't you bring a bottle of wine with you and we can stay in by the fire?'

Tom agreed and then muttering something about a lecture, disappeared.

The carpet fitters arrived as promised and set to work at once. Petra had decided to close carpet both the bedroom and the living-room this time. The salt water had badly stained the polished wooden floor in the living-room and utterly destroyed the rugs.

When Tom arrived he was full of admiration for the work she and the students had done.

'It really does look lovely,' he said as he made the guided tour. 'I see the bed wasn't harmed.'

Petra had an almost overwhelming desire to giggle, but she managed to keep her countenance and say, 'The water stained the legs and took all the polish off, of course, but luckily it didn't reach the mattress. Mrs. Arden sat on it until we were rescued — it gave her somewhere dry.'

'Have you seen her since the flood?' Tom asked as they went back into the living-room. 'Where's a corkscrew? I'll open this wine.'

Petra found it for him and said, 'No. She was in a nursing-home for a while and now she's moved into an old folks' home. Nicholas moved her on Saturday.'

Tom poured the wine and handed her a glass. 'I really am very sorry about Saturday evening,' he began.

Petra interrupted him. 'Yes, you said so, Tom. Let's forget it.'

'Petra, I can't. I was drunk and . . . '

'I know,' she said drily.

'But do you know why? Why I'd set out to drink myself under the table? Because I was insanely jealous.' He set his glass down and said aggressively, 'I love you, Petra. You must know I do.' He moved to take her in his arms but she pulled free saying, 'I didn't, Tom, we just had fun, that's all. I'm sorry, I really didn't know how you felt.'

'Well you must be blind, that's all.' Tom was almost shouting and Petra was suddenly afraid.

'Tom,' she said as calmly as she could, 'I'm sorry if I hurt you. I really am. I'm very fond of you, you know that . . . '

'Fond!' growled Tom. 'How very generous of you.' He grabbed hold of her and forced her to face him. 'Fond's no good to me, Petra. I came here to ask you to marry me.'

'Well, you're making a pretty poor job of it,' said Petra with spirit. 'Please let go of me, Tom.'

His hands slid from her arms, and he said miserably, 'I am, aren't I? Can I start again?'

Petra replied as gently as she could, disturbed by his dejected expression, 'No, Tom. It'd be better if you didn't.

I'm truly sorry if you feel this way and I hate you to be hurt because of me, but I can't give you more. I love you dearly as a friend, but that's all.'

'A friend,' said Tom bitterly. 'When I want to love you! I could make you love me, Petra. If you'd only let me make love to you properly, you'd see.'

* * *

Petra, who had relaxed her guard a little as Tom had calmed down, suddenly found herself snatched into his arms once more. Holding her with a strength she found it impossible to break from, he forced his mouth on hers, kissing her brutally, pushing her back against the wall so that her body was crushed against his. She fought him, struggling to free herself and all of a sudden he let go.

'Don't worry,' he sneered. 'I'm not going to force you. I wouldn't, anyway, in the same place *he* did last Saturday. Oh, I know you didn't go back to your room in college, so you needn't pretend.'

As suddenly as before his manner changed. 'Oh, Petra, wouldn't you rather be with a real man who can show you what love really is, someone who's free to love you and marry you and give you children, than — ' his expression darkened again — 'a man who's married and would have to keep you tucked away and then leave you alone while he scuttles back home to his darling wife?'

Petra stared at Tom in blank disbelief. The colour drained from her face leaving her pale and cold. 'But — but Nicholas isn't married,' she whispered.

'Isn't he? Have you asked him?'

'No, of course not. The subject . . . '

'Didn't arise.' Tom finished the sentence for her. 'I'm sure it didn't! He'd take care of that, at least until he was sure of you.'

Petra's legs felt weak and she sank on to a chair. 'I don't believe you,' she said. 'You're making it up just to get your own back. I know you are!'

Tom laughed unpleasantly. 'I might have, if I'd thought of it. But in this case I didn't have to. Nicholas Romilly is married, so there's no room for you in his life except as his mistress.'

'How do you know he's married?' asked Petra, a little of her spirit returning to her. 'Who told you?'

'No one told me, but it's not difficult to find out. You gave me a book of his to read before he came to the conference. Well, I didn't read it then, but I have now, at least — ' he corrected himself smoothly — 'I've read the jacket and that's the most interesting part of all. I'll show you.'

To Petra's horror he picked up his discarded overcoat and took a book from its pocket. She recognised it at once as a copy of one of Nicholas' accounts of some work he'd done on the Greek mainland several years before.

Tom presented it to her open at the back where the author's notes were on the jacket. There was a list of Nicholas' scholastic achievements including his chair at a new university and then at the end the words she had been dreading leapt to meet her: '*Professor Romilly lives with his wife in London*.'

Petra stared unseeing at the words. Tears filled her eyes and poured down her cheeks. Silently she wept, in sudden and awful desolation. The hand that held the book shook violently and Tom took it from her.

For a moment he watched her, all triumph draining away as he saw her grief, then he said softly, 'Do you want me to stay?'

Unable to speak, Petra shook her head, she wanted to be alone. Gently he kissed her forehead and turned away.

Petra didn't recoil at his kiss, she was unaware of it, as she was unaware of his departure. It wasn't until the click of the latch on the front door penetrated her mind that she knew he had gone and rending sobs escaped her.

* * *

Petra arrived at college the next morning very pale and washed-out but with a great many things sorted out in her mind. She hadn't slept that night. For the first few hours she lay on the bed where she had been with Nicholas and wept for her lost happiness. Her life seemed to stretch away into the distance, a flat grey expanse without relief or colour. She viewed it bleakly for a long time before her natural optimism exerted itself in any measure.

Pale-faced, Petra had returned to the living-room and picked up the book. There once again she read the fateful words. Turning to the front she looked for the date of publication and discovered it was 1978. Seven years ago. A flame of hope flickered inside her. All that Tom had proved from the book was that Nicholas had been married in 1977, but it was now 1985 and anything might have happened. People got divorced, didn't they? Or died? Petra shuddered. She didn't wish anybody dead, not even Nicholas' wife, but marriages did break up.

Why hadn't Nicholas said at the outset that he was married? Why hadn't he brought his wife to the conference? Why hadn't the subject come up in conversation? Was that what he'd been going to tell her before their feelings had blotted out all thoughts of speech?

All these questions churned in her mind, and yet she was no nearer a solution. How could she confirm the situation one way or another? One answer was obvious and that was to tax Nicholas with it on Saturday, but even as her mind accepted this as the simple solution she was loath to do so without further proof. It wasn't so long ago that she had accused Nicholas of inhuman and uncivilised behaviour without making enough effort to check the facts and circumstances. She had been made to look a fool then, and she was in no hurry to make the same mistake again.

Perhaps Nicholas had just assumed she knew the truth. If he thought she already knew, then there was no need to say anything to her. He hadn't necessarily set out to deceive her.

Then she recalled again how he had put her away from him on two earlier occasions. How he had kissed her passionately and then broken free as if something had come into his mind — memories of his wife? She could call to mind now the strange torment on his face in the car; as if he were fighting a battle, she had thought at the time. Perhaps he had been, against his guilt.

And when he left her curled up in bed, saying he had commitments in Yorkshire, had he really had to be there that day or did he have to return home to spend Sunday with his wife first?

But if there was a wife waiting patiently at home, where did she think he had been on Saturday? The answer to that particular question was simple of course: he'd been in Grayston-on-Sea moving his mother into an old people's home.

* * *

None of the questions which bombarded Petra's bemused brain brought her any nearer to resolving the situation, but as the grey dawn crept into the sky, she managed to make one firm decision. She would find later books in the college library or better still look in *Who's Who*. A man like Professor Nicholas Romilly would almost certainly be in that.

Even this minor decision helped her feel a little better, and she made herself a cup of coffee and, still feeling unable to sleep, set to work on assessing the students' essays she had brought home the previous evening.

She fought to concentrate her mind on the work in front of her, but even so she found her thoughts drifting away from studies of the Paston letters and the fifteenth-century, and returning to the dull ache in her heart which told her her hopes were indeed forlorn ones and that Nicholas was indeed married.

Well, she would make what enquiries she could and then tackle Nicholas when he came on Saturday. If he came.

There was no time before her first lecture to visit the library, but when it was over she hurried to the reference section and searched for *Who's Who*.

She carried the hefty tome across to a quiet table in an alcove and with trembling fingers turned up *Romilly — Peregrine Nicholas b. 25th June 1948* — then his schools were listed and universities and then in black and white *m. Anne Chapple 1973*. More information followed, but Petra didn't read it. *Who's Who* thought he was married as well, and now the wife had a name. Anne. Quickly she checked the date of that edition. 1980, still not completely up to date.

Her flame of hope refused to be quenched. Surely someone like Nicholas would not two-time his wife, he was a man of integrity, wasn't he? In public life yes, in private who knew? Several of the girl students had been in raptures about him, and certainly not with regard to his lecture and his work alone.

He was an extremely attractive man. Surely he'd have no difficulty finding willing women if he wanted them. 'Witness the way I fell swooning into his arms,' thought Petra bitterly, but even so she couldn't believe it of him. Not yet. All that was left to her was to ask him outright — but then if it weren't true, she would have admitted that she had doubted him; believed him capable of such duplicity. And if it did turn out to be true, he would surely laugh at her naïveté. Not that that would matter very much, she thought dully, for I shouldn't see him again if it were true. So she told herself and so she had decided, but that decision had yet to be put to the test.

Then, while she was in the middle of a tutorial, an idea came to her and the simplicity of it made her feel quite faint. As soon as the session was over, she reached for her briefcase and emptied it on to her desk. Quickly she searched through the papers and files until she found what she was looking for, the letter from Nicholas accepting the invitation to speak at the conference. There at the top was printed his London address and phone number. There was one easy way to confirm or deny the truth of Nicholas being married and that was to phone and see if his wife answered.

She shoved the letter into her handbag and spent the rest of the day going through the motions of being a lecturer and tutor. She didn't see Tom. She had no wish to meet him with things still unresolved and so she made coffee in her tutorial room and kept well clear of the staffroom and dining-hall. Nor did Tom make any effort to seek her out, for which she was grateful.

At last the day ended. Another of her decisions, that of moving back into the flat immediately, had to be implemented and ringing for a taxi she packed her belongings and vacated the college guest-room. She left a note of thanks for the Principal, remembering to commend, in it, the students who had so generously come to her aid, and waited for the taxi in the hall.

* * *

When at last Petra was safely in the refuge of her home, she made herself a pot of tea and then, finding herself unable to do anything until she had made her phone call, she drew the letter with his number on it from her handbag, and prepared to dial.

The number rang out and as she listened, praying that no Mrs. Romilly would answer it, Petra suddenly wondered what she would say if there was a reply — she had thought of no excuse for the call.

Quickly she slammed her hand on the telephone buttons and cut off the call. She must have a reason to phone. She thought for a moment, to find something that, should it be needed, would not arouse Nicholas' suspicions if he heard of the call later. Journalist? No, she would have to name a paper.

Business? Market Research? Then a perfect idea came to her, she would say she was a freelance photographer and ask to make an appointment to take some pictures. Nicholas wasn't there, of course, so she could ring off promising to call again for an appointment.

Once again she dialled the number, promising herself she would wait for twenty rings before she rang off. There was no reply. Instead of adding fuel to her hopes this inconclusive result made her even more depressed. She rang again every twenty minutes, each time letting the number ring twenty times before giving up.

At her fifth attempt, on the eleventh ring, the receiver was picked up and a woman with a pleasant voice said the number. Shaking violently, Petra took a deep breath and began her prepared call.

'Is that Professor Nicholas Romilly's home?'

'Yes, it is, who's calling, please?'

'May I speak to Professor Romilly, please?'

'I'm sorry, he's in Yorkshire this week.' The voice sounded regretful.

'Am I speaking to Mrs. Romilly?' asked Petra huskily.

'Yes.'

'Mrs. Anne Romilly?'

'That's right. Who is that, please?'

'I'm so sorry to trouble you, Mrs. Romilly, my name is — ' Petra paused, she hadn't thought of a name, 'Margaret Mitchell — ' she had caught sight of her copy of *Gone with the Wind*, on the bookshelf. 'I'm a freelance photographer. I just wanted to make an appointment with Professor Romilly. Perhaps I can phone again.'

'Yes, do, Miss Mitchell. I expect him home tomorrow evening.'

'Thank you very much,' and feeling sick and miserable, Petra hung up.

Anne Romilly had existed in 1978 when the book was published, in 1980 when the *Who's Who* in the library was published and in 1985 when Petra Hinton spoke to her on the telephone.

7

Now that she had established beyond doubt that Nicholas, the man she had fallen so deeply in love with, was married, Petra, stunned and shocked, had to consider what she should do about the situation.

She could of course tell him she knew about his wife and say she would never see him again. That was indeed what she knew she ought to do, but had she the strength? Supposing he admitted he was married when she taxed him with it, but suggested they carried on their own liaison? Was she prepared to do so? Was half a loaf better than no bread? Or, she could pretend she knew nothing and wait for him to tell her, but even then the ultimate question to be decided would be the same.

The evening stretched before her, but

there was work she had to do, and trying hard to relegate all thoughts of Nicholas and her dilemma to the back of her mind, she set herself to it. She was in some measure successful. Even though as she closed each folder she had to force herself to open the next, while she was actually reading the contents and commenting upon them, she found her attention held.

At last she closed the final one and went to bed. She pulled her quilt about her and dozed off quite quickly despite her mind's subconscious agonising about her problems.

When she awoke in the morning she felt tired and unrested, but she found her decision had been partially taken. She would tell Nicholas she knew about his wife. She knew there was no way she could maintain a pretence of not knowing. All she had to do was wait for a suitable moment on Saturday night and break the news.

All she could do now, was live

through the next thirty-six hours, and as always hard work seemed the answer. After a morning of third year lectures and tutorials, she got ready to pay an unexpected visit on her teaching practice students. It would keep her mind well occupied and mean she would have little chance of meeting Tom.

On her way past the secretary's office, she popped in to hand in her expenses sheet. Miss Merton, the secretary, was a chatty soul, and Petra was subjected to the latest college gossip, all except that relating to herself, of course.

Miss Merton was interrupted in full flow when the telephone rang, and Petra edged thankfully away as the secretary's attention was turned from her, but she was stopped at the door.

'This call's for you, Petra. Don't be too long, your friends should use the common-room phone, you know.'

* * *

Petra's heart missed a beat. It must be Nicholas. No one else would ring her here. She was right and her heart skipped again as she heard his deep voice say, 'Petra? Is that you? I thought I'd have to leave a message.'

Aware that Miss Merton was at her elbow, gathering in every word for future distribution, Petra kept her reply formal.

'Yes, Professor, how nice to hear from you.'

Nicholas laughed. 'You're being overheard,' he said.

'As a matter of fact I am.'

'Never mind. We'll cut the protestations of undying love to a minimum. Had a good week?'

'Not bad. Have you?' Petra found her voice came huskily and cleared her throat.

'Fine. Very good, in fact. The problem is, as a result, something has come up and I shan't be able to make it this weekend.'

'Oh.'

'I'm sorry, angel, but I'll try and get away one day next week.'

'If you like.' Petra suddenly felt very tired.

'Sure you don't mind?' Nicholas sounded relieved.

'No. I understand.'

'I knew you would. I'll explain it all when I see you.'

'Yes. I must go now.' Petra knew it sounded rather abrupt, but she had to end the conversation before she broke down and cried.

Nicholas' voice softened. 'Take care. I'll come as soon as I can get away. 'Bye now.'

''Bye.' Petra's farewell was little more than a whisper and she replaced the receiver.

With a deep breath she turned round to face the inquisitive secretary. 'Thank you, Miss Merton,' she said and left the office.

So, Nicholas wasn't coming on Saturday and Petra would have to wait even longer before she could have an answer to the question that tormented her. His words, 'couldn't get away,' came back to her, echoing in her despondent mind. 'Get away,' as if there was a restriction.

Quickly she made a decision and before setting out to visit her students as she had planned, she slipped into the telephone booth in the front hall and phoned her parents.

'Darling, what a lovely surprise,' cried her mother. 'Of course you can come home for the weekend. When shall we expect you?'

'I'll collect my things after college this afternoon,' Petra replied, 'and depending on trains, should be with you later tonight.'

'That's marvellous,' said her mother. 'Dad will be pleased when I tell him. I'll have something in the oven that'll keep, so just get here when you can.'

Her mother's voice sounded so relaxed and normal that Petra almost broke down, but she knew she had made the right decision. A weekend alone in the flat was unthinkable.

* * *

She made her school visit brief and managed to catch a train earlier than she had anticipated. Once she was on her way, Petra found herself longing to be there, close within the safe familiarity of home, with her parents, always so loving and understanding at her side. They would know at once, when they saw her, that something was wrong, but Petra was certain they wouldn't pry or question her; they would wait for her to confide in them. If she chose not to, they would give her comfort and strength simply by being there.

In this Petra was right. Apart from commenting that Petra looked pale and in need of a good night's sleep, her mother said nothing to show that she was aware of Petra's low spirits.

Petra herself very nearly did pour out

the whole story to her mother. Several times she was on the point of speaking, but on each occasion she drew back. The decision she had to make was one she had to make alone. She knew how her parents would view her involvement with a married man and as the two days of the weekend progressed, the standards and values instilled into her since she had been a child asserted themselves once more and she knew what her decision must be.

Having made her choice Petra knew she must implement it at once, before her strength failed her and she changed her mind. Borrowing a sheet of notepaper from her mother that Sunday afternoon, she wrote to Nicholas and told him she didn't want to see him again. She gave no reason but asked him to respect her decision as final and not to contact her again. She read the letter through once and miserably dry-eyed, sent it to the address at the head of his own letter.

'I think I'll walk along and post this,'

she said as casually as she could.

Her mother looked at the threatening sky and said, ‘Do you really want to go now? It won’t go till tomorrow, you know.’

Petra felt certain that if the letter was still in her possession tomorrow it wouldn’t go at all, so she said, ‘I shan’t be long, but I could do with a breath of fresh air and a walk after that enormous lunch.’

The sky fulfilled its promise and by the time she reached the post office, the rain was coming down hard, pounding on the pavement, bouncing several inches into the air. Petra was drenched in moments, but she was hardly aware of the fact. With rain running down her face, her own tears passed unnoticed; her mind was already cold, her body reaching the same state seemed unimportant.

‘Goodbye, Nicholas,’ she whispered and slipped her letter into the box. Then she continued to walk in the rain until weariness took her home. Despite the dreadful emptiness that stretched before her, Petra felt more at ease with herself, calmer and more relaxed than she had since Tom had first told her about Nicholas.

Something of it showed in her face, for when she finally reached her parents' house and stood dripping on the hall carpet, her mother simply put her arms round her for a moment and said, 'I don't know what decision you've been making, darling, but I'm sure you've made the right one.' She hugged Petra fiercely and added, 'Go and have a bath before you catch your death of cold, then when we've had tea, Dad and I'll drive you back to the flat. No trains for you tonight.'

Petra was supremely grateful for her mother's understanding, and managed to maintain some semblance of normality until they had seen her into the flat, but when at last the front door closed behind them and she was left alone in the silence of her room, Petra crept into bed, the bed where she had found such joy, and cried herself to sleep.

* * *

Nicholas Romilly's reaction to Petra's letter was characteristically swift and decisive. He ignored her requests not to come again and to accept this as final and arrived on her doorstep on Tuesday evening.

Petra, knowing Nicholas, had feared he would do just that and had prepared herself to face him, so it was no surprise, when a thundering fist summoned her to her door, to find Nicholas waiting outside.

Without a word he strode past her through the flat into the living-room. Petra closed the door behind him and taking a deep breath followed him. He stood with his back to the windows, for all the world as he had stood in the basement flat the first time she had seen him, and as she entered the room he dragged her letter, crumpled from his pocket.

‘What is this?’ he asked, his voice tight and controlled.

Petra looked across at him and replied calmly, ‘I imagine it’s the letter I wrote you.’ She felt far from calm, but she was determined not to fight with him, nor to break down and cry.

‘What does it mean?’ he demanded.

‘Exactly what it says,’ she replied carefully. ‘You shouldn’t have come here.’

‘Aren’t I at least entitled to some explanation?’ he said coldly. ‘I had a feeling perhaps that our last evening together might have given me a right to that.’

Petra had guessed that if Nicholas came at all he would demand an explanation, and she had prepared one for him. The idea of giving him the true explanation — that she had discovered he was married — she had quickly dismissed. If his marriage had not proved a barrier from his point of view before, there was no reason to expect it to do so now, and Petra had an awful feeling that if he took it into his head to try and persuade her to carry on the affair, she might well fall prey to the temptation.

So she had an explanation ready and now she began to give it, but under the dark glare of his eyes she faltered and didn't deliver the speech as she had rehearsed it.

'I don't want to see you again because I'm going to marry Tom.' She blurted it out and then shrank away from him as she saw the fury mounting in his face.

'And when was this all arranged?' His voice was soft and low and chilling.

'We've — we've been going out together for some time and, well, when he saw us together at Angelo's he discovered how jealous it made him and realised he was in love with me.' Petra's words tumbled out under Nicholas' icy stare.

'And that was the object of the exercise? To make him jealous?'

* * *

Faced with the angry expression she had hoped would never be directed at her, Petra could only nod dumbly.

'And your little bit of play-acting did the trick, did it? Next day he rushed round and popped the question?' Nicholas spoke contemptuously, his face a mask of disgust. 'How delighted you must be that your ruse worked. Of course, I'd have thought the latter part of the evening a little over and above the call of duty, unless of course Tom was in the wings somewhere.'

'Nicholas!' The cry was ripped from her at his cruelty, but she knew she had achieved her object. After this confrontation there was no way Nicholas Romilly would approach her again.

'Nicholas!' he mimicked. 'I might not have minded bringing your Tom to his senses, my dear, had you confided the purpose of the exercise to me. But I dislike being used.'

'So do I,' said Petra miserably.

'I dare say we all do,' said Nicholas smoothly. 'And when is the happy day?'

'I don't know yet.'

Something in the way she spoke made Nicholas jerk his eyes to her face once more. 'Surely Tom is eager to claim his bride; the bride who maintained he *had* no claim to her only a week ago? Or doesn't he know yet?'

'I — I,' began Petra, quailing under his gaze.

'He doesn't know yet!' cried Nicholas with an unpleasant bark of laughter. 'You haven't accepted him yet, have you?' He grabbed Petra by the shoulders and shook her hard. 'You were waiting to see if I could come up with a better offer. Well, sorry to disappoint you, darling, but I can't. Tom Davies is welcome to you. You deserve each other.' He thrust her from him in disgust and without a backward glance, strode from the room. The slam of the front door found an answering echo in Petra's heart as it too closed on an empty silence.

* * *

For several weeks Petra moved and lived as if in a dream. Every day she went to college, delivered her lectures, held her tutorials, helped her teaching practice students through their final days. Outwardly she was calm, inwardly she was cold. No emotion seemed to touch her; her laughter was a mechanical reaction, lacking spontaneity; her eyes were dry.

On one occasion she was jerked from her lethargy, only to be plunged in deeper as a result. She thought about Mrs. Arden, now safely established in the old people's home and decided she ought to go and see her. Suppressing in her mind that the reason for this was that Mrs. Arden was the only tenuous link she had with Nicholas, Petra telephoned the home and spoke to the warden.

'My dear, I'm so sorry,' said the warden in dismay. 'Mrs. Arden died last week. A heart attack. Her funeral was yesterday.'

Petra was staggered. 'Oh, I see. I didn't know.'

'Who did you say you are?'

'Just a friend. I used to live in the same house. I did her shopping sometimes.'

'I'm so sorry you weren't told of her death,' said the troubled warden. 'Her son was told and he made all the arrangements. He can't have realised. He was at the crematorium of course, but they didn't stay. It was a very quiet affair.'

'They?' queried Petra.

'He and a woman, his wife perhaps? He didn't introduce us.'

'No. Well, thank you for telling me. Goodbye.' Petra replaced the receiver. Her last link with Nicholas Romilly was gone. Mrs. Arden was dead and buried, and he hadn't even bothered to let Petra know. Anger sparked for a moment and then the torpor settled back once more.

* * *

Petra stopped avoiding Tom. It was not his fault that his words had been true, and she had long since forgiven him the way he had broken the news to her. And Tom, seeing she no longer avoided him, sought her out and tentatively offered his friendship once again.

Because she was lonely and it didn't matter, Petra accepted his company and might eventually have accepted more; but the term drew to a close and the holidays caused a natural break in their relationship. Tom went skiing over the Easter holiday and Petra visited an old college friend, Mary, in Cumbria. Mary was happily married to a Cumbrian farmer and Petra slipped into the farm routine with an ease that amazed her. The wild freedom of the fells crept into her soul and in the bright days of early April she braved the chill of the hillside air and the sudden downpours of the rain and strode out across the hillsides as if in search of something. Mary was so happy with her husband Clive, that at first Petra felt she was intruding, but theirs was a relationship apart, complete when they were alone, elastic enough to include those round them with ease when they were not and Petra envied them.

One afternoon, soon after Easter, Petra and Mary were alone in the farm kitchen. As they worked together on a mammoth baking session for the freezer, Petra began to tell Mary about Nicholas.

She had spoken of him to no one since the night he had flung her from him in disgust and the telling of the tale was like the lancing of a boil.

Mary paused at her work and listened as all the bitterness, humiliation and misery came pouring out. She was far enough removed from the situation for Petra to hold nothing back. Mary knew neither of the men involved and could make no judgment, all she did was to listen until Petra had no more to tell.

'Where is he now?' Mary asked at last. 'Back with his wife?'

Petra shrugged her shoulders wearily. 'I suppose so. I mean, he never left her, did he?'

'And Tom? What about him?'

'He's skiing in Austria.'

'Yes, I know, I didn't mean that.' Mary looked at her friend with sympathetic eyes. 'What I meant was, what is he to you?'

'A friend.'

'And no more?'

Petra sighed. 'I don't know, Mary. I suppose he could be more; in time. I was very fond of him before all this blew up. I expect I could be again, given time.'

Mary leaned over and took her friend's hand. 'Don't settle for second best, Petra,' she said earnestly. 'It's never worth it. Only marry Tom if you really want him, otherwise wait. Someone else will come along who'll make you forget the both of them.'

Petra smiled. 'I'm a little past the 'tall dark stranger' bit,' she said.

'Rubbish,' replied Mary with asperity.

'No one is. Clive and I met and were married within three months. I'm a firm believer in love at first sight.'

'So am I,' agreed Petra laughing, but her thoughts were not of a stranger.

* * *

Having at last confided in someone, Petra felt better than she had for weeks. Somehow the stress had lessened and she spent the last few days of her time in Cumbria far more at peace with herself and returned to Grayston-on-Sea rested and ready for the summer term.

Tom returned too and lost no time in seeking Petra out. He found her in the staff-room a few days before term opened and insisted on carrying her off to the Admiral for a drink.

Once he had her seated in a corner, a large gin and tonic in front of her, he sat down and beamed at her. He was so different from the slightly apologetic Tom who had taken her out at the end of the spring term, that she could only stare at him in amazement. The Easter weather had been good in the mountains, and Tom, skiing at heights of nine and ten thousand feet, had caught the sun so that his face was darkly tanned. But it wasn't so much his healthy tan that surprised Petra, it was his perpetual grin and shining eyes.

'Come on, out with it,' she said when he had sat down beside her. 'You look like the cat that's got the cream.'

Tom's grin broadened even more. 'Cheers!' he said.

'Cheers. Come on, Tom,' cried Petra, 'or I shall die of curiosity.'

'When I was skiing,' he began, 'I went into ski school and there was this girl, Melanie.' His voice lingered on her name and at once Petra knew what was coming.

'Tom?' she said, a question in her voice.

He nodded. 'You must congratulate me, Petra. I'm getting married.'

'Married!' The word was surprised from her.

'I thought you'd be surprised.' Tom beamed and then suddenly realising that he was talking to the girl he had proposed to not three months before, added awkwardly, 'You don't mind, Petra, do you? I mean there was never anything between us really, was there?'

Petra managed to smile reassuringly. 'Only friendship, Tom. I told you once I was very fond of you and I still am, but I don't love you in the marrying way.'

The faint clouding cleared from Tom's expression and he said, 'I'm glad. I'd hate to have hurt you again.'

Anxious not to begin on that subject, Petra said quickly, 'Tell me about Melanie.'

Tom needed no second invitation, and by the time they left the pub Petra felt she had known Melanie for years.

'The trouble is,' he confided as they walked back to college, 'Melanie being so far away. I mean it'll be a long journey for one of us every weekend, so we decided that the sooner we got married the better.'

'Have you set a date already?' Petra was surprised.

'Yes.' Tom beamed. 'At Whitsun.'

Petra was even more surprised. She had expected him to name a date in the long summer vacation.

'That's awfully quick, Tom,' she said anxiously. 'Are you quite certain of yourself?'

Tom stopped walking and turned to her, his grey eyes serious. 'I have never been more certain of anything in my life,' he said quietly. He smiled then, a little ruefully. 'Oh, I know I said I loved you, Petra, but I'm sure you won't be offended if I say it was never what I feel for Melanie. That is entirely different.'

'I do know, Tom,' she said softly.

Tom took her hand. 'Of course you do, I'm sorry.'

* * *

Miss Danvers was waiting for Petra when they returned. 'Ah, there you are, Petra,' she said. 'I've been looking for you. There's something we must discuss. Can you spare me a minute now?'

'Of course, Miss Danvers,' and Petra followed the senior lecturer into her tutorial room.

Miss Danvers waved her to a chair. 'The Principal and I feel that when we offer the short course options to the second years at the end of this term, we might include a six week introduction to archaeology. Professor Romilly set the scene so well with his lecture at the conference last term, I think we might find it was a popular option. How does it strike you?'

Petra was shaken by the unexpectedness of the suggestion. She hadn't considered trying to follow up Nicholas' lecture. She stared, unseeing, out of the window for a moment, her heart beating fast as if she had been actually confronted with the man rather than just his work; then she took command of herself once more and said, 'I'm sure it would, Miss Danvers. Do you want me to run it?'

Miss Danvers smiled. 'I think that would be just the thing, if you don't mind the extra work.'

'No,' Petra assured her. 'I don't mind. I'm sure I shall enjoy it.'

They discussed the framework of the course and Petra promised to have a more detailed scheme of work ready to present to Miss Danvers within a week or two; then they parted and Petra went off to the library before going home.

It really had been a day of surprises, she thought; first Tom's news and now a new course to run, and though tenuous, she still had a link with Nicholas.

The course, as outlined by Miss Danvers, was to be very general, but the selection of archaeological books Petra took from the library to prepare her work contained several of his works. 'It's a pity he's only just beginning work on the Thessos book,' she thought.

'Having heard him speak on the subject, I know it'd be the most interesting of all.'

* * *

As soon as the students returned, Petra had little time to herself. As always she worked long and hard and without her being conscious of the passing of time the days slipped away.

It was one day not long before the Whitsun break that she came home to find the door to the basement flat open. Staring at it, Petra's heart began to pound. Why was the door ajar? Was there someone down there? Could it be Nicholas?

Quietly, she eased the door wider and pausing on the top step, listened. There was the sound of movement below, someone was definitely down there.

Petra clutched at the banister rail, the hope that it might be Nicholas welled up inside her, overpowering all claims of reason. She ached to see him, and the ache was as strong as on the day he'd gone. Nothing would have prevented her from going down those stairs and as she did so the blood was singing in her ears. The sounds below were quite distinct now, but when Petra entered the living-room it wasn't Nicholas she found there but a stranger.

The precious hope drained away leaving her empty and lost.

'Hello,' said the man. 'Did you want someone?'

Petra explained that she had seen the door open and had come down to investigate.

'I live upstairs,' she said, 'and I hold a spare key.'

'Oh, I see,' the man nodded. 'Well, we've been instructed to sell the place, so you'll be having new neighbours.'

'Are you an agent?' asked Petra.

'Yes. Here's my authorisation and business card.'

Petra studied them then said, 'I'd better give you the key I have.' She took it from her handbag and handed it to him.

'Thanks.' He slipped it on to a key ring. 'There, it's with ours now. I'll pass it on when I give ours back. We'll be bringing people to view, of course.'

'Yes, of course.'

As Petra went back up to her own flat, she recognised the usual empty feeling inside her that still recurred every time she allowed herself to think of Nicholas.

'This is ridiculous,' she thought. 'I haven't seen him for several months and he still has this effect on me. Perhaps if I did try and see him I'd find he wasn't at all as I remembered.'

She dismissed this last idea as impractical. There was no way in which she could meet Nicholas casually and she had no intention of manufacturing a meeting. She realised then how much she had been wishing Nicholas would need to return to his mother's flat for something; how much she had been clinging to this hope, so that she might see him again, and now with the arrival of the estate agent that last chance was gone. There was nothing to bring Nicholas anywhere near her.

8

The day of Tom's wedding dawned bright and clear. He was married in Warwickshire where Melanie lived, and Petra had borrowed her father's car and travelled up the night before. She stayed in the village pub, a charming timbered building, and when she woke in the morning and found the summer sun streaming through the leaded window panes her spirits rose and she got up determined to enjoy herself.

It was a big wedding. Melanie's parents were determined to give their only daughter a magnificent send-off. When she arrived at the church in a lace wedding gown that floated round her in a mist of white, attended by three small bridesmaids in buttercup crinolines, Petra, turning with the rest of the congregation, found tears in her eyes.

Melanie was radiant, and as she

walked up the aisle on her father's arm, Petra looked across at Tom. He had stepped forward to meet his bride and the look in his eyes spoke eloquently of his feelings for her. Petra knew then that Tom had been right when he said that he had absolutely no doubts about marrying Melanie.

The reception was held at a local hotel and was a noisy, joyful affair. Petra knew several of Tom's friends, and once they realised she was not heartbroken by his marriage to Melanie, all constraints vanished and they made a convivial group. But when the bride and groom had left for their honeymoon, Petra suddenly found she needed to be alone. Smilingly she declined an offer to go on to a party in Birmingham with the excuse that she had to return her father's car, and thankfully escaped.

Cruising steadily down the motorway, she was glad she had arranged to spend the rest of the holiday weekend with her parents. The first half of term had been very tiring, and the second half, with the extra archaeological course, threatened to be even more so.

She spent a comfortable evening with her parents and as the hands of the clock showed ten-thirty she yawned. 'I think I'll go up to bed now,' she said.

'Will you?' said her father. 'I thought I'd watch that Saturday chat show tonight. I think you might enjoy it, Petra. That archaeologist chap who did your lecture for you, is appearing.'

Petra slumped back into her chair. 'Nicholas Romilly?' Her voice came out uncertainly, but her father didn't seem to notice.

'That's the one,' he said cheerfully. 'But don't stay up if you're tired. I just thought it might interest you.'

'Yes,' answered Petra, trying to sound casual. 'I think it might. I told you I've got to do the archaeology course soon, so it might be a help.'

* * *

Nicholas was the third guest to be interviewed and so Petra had to sit through the first half hour of the programme trying not to show her feelings. Her mind was in turmoil, here was the chance she had wanted, a chance to see him again and perhaps discover she was only remembering a dream, not the man himself. Part of her was determined to find that this was indeed the case, but the rest of her, her pounding heart and aching body, played her false and the mere anticipation of seeing him again, even if only on television, made her feel weak.

At last he came on, tall, dark-eyed as she had remembered and as magnetic as ever. His smile, as always, brought his mobile face to life making him seem younger than his thirty-seven years. He looked thinner, his muscles more tightly drawn than she remembered, but otherwise he was just the same and Petra's heart contracted painfully at the sight of him.

After a brief introduction, he was

asked about his work.

'Well,' began Nicholas, 'I've been extremely lucky recently. While I was in Yorkshire on a brief lecture tour earlier this year, I met up with some people who were prepared to sponsor my latest project.' He went on to describe his work on Thessos and told again the legend of the lonely princess.

'This sponsorship will enable me to continue my work on the site. And for that I'm immeasurably grateful.'

'Well, Nicholas,' drawled the interviewer, 'I gather you're off to Thessos very soon now.'

'Yes, I've just completed writing up my findings so far . . . '

'In a book you mean?'

'As the basis for my next book, yes. But as I'm going back, I'm hoping there will be a great deal more information to add.'

Petra watched him, her eyes devouring his face, her ears straining to memorise the sound of his deep voice. What he actually said flowed over her and as the interviewer mentioned his earlier career she paid little attention to the words.

Once she let her eyes flicker to her parents' faces and found them as caught up in what Nicholas was saying as the students had been at his lecture; then something he said did penetrate her mind, at first filtering through slowly and then stabbing her into painful consciousness like the fierce jab of a needle. The interviewer had asked why he had given up the archaeological chair he had held at the university and returned full time to field work and writing.

Nicholas considered a moment before replying, 'It was when my wife, Anne, was killed in 1980.' For a moment his face clouded over and then he said, 'Until then I was happy being based here in England — I enjoyed the teaching and home was there at the end of the day. We travelled a good deal of course, and I was involved in various projects, but we kept our home as a private retreat that we could come back to.' He paused again before saying, 'After the crash I couldn't face living in the house alone. I decided to alter my way of life completely, so I resigned and went back to work in the field.' He smiled. 'When I'm in England I stay with my mother and work from there. She's one of my sternest critics, I might add.'

The interview lasted another five minutes, but Petra heard none of it. The words, 'When my wife, Anne, was killed,' pierced her brain and the blood seemed to rush to her head, thundering, deafening so that Petra felt she must drown in the sound. She felt sick and giddy and the world tilted round her. Her fingers clutched the arms of her chair and her knuckles turned white as she fought to keep herself from crumpling into an undignified heap on the floor.

As her father switched off the television at the end of the programme, Petra's mother said, 'I should go up now, darling. You're looking really pale and tired. Don't get up in the morning, have a good lie in and I'll bring you breakfast in bed.'

⋆ ⋆ ⋆

Somehow Petra got to her feet and in a strange calm voice bid her parents good night. Somehow she got upstairs to her own bedroom, warm and snug and waiting for her.

She dragged herself on to her bed and lay staring at the ceiling, her mind whirling at the news she had just heard and the implications of it. Nicholas wasn't married, not any more. His wife, Anne, the Anne Chapple mentioned in *Who's Who* had been killed in a crash of some sort in 1980. Nicholas was free. Nicholas was free. The woman who had answered the phone must have been his stepmother, Mrs. Romilly indeed, but Mrs. Romilly senior.

Her heart leapt within her, but even as it did so her hopes came crashing round her ears. Nicholas might well be free, but similarly he might not. It was months since she had seen him, he could well have found someone else. And Nicholas thought she was married to Tom, or about to be. How could she tell him? Why hadn't she asked him about his wife? If only she had said, 'Tom says you're married. Is it true?' But she hadn't and she'd lied to him and she'd sent him away. And it was all her fault.

Tears oozed out from beneath her lids as she remembered his face — the tenderness and wonder as they'd shared their love, the cold fury and contempt when she had told him she was marrying Tom. Would he ever forgive her if she went to him and told him everything? Would he want her back anyway or had he forgotten her in the arms of somebody else? If anything could be done it was she who must do it. It was clear Nicholas had no intention of approaching her again. Quite apart from the fact that he thought her engaged or married to Tom Davies, there was his pride.

'But I have no pride where you're concerned, Nicholas,' she whispered to the empty room. 'Seeing you tonight made me realise how much I love you still, and hearing what you said has given me another chance. Will you let me come to you?'

* * *

Even as she spoke her thoughts aloud, Petra remembered he had never said he loved her, never spoken of love; but she couldn't forget how he had wanted her, nor the passion with which he had taken her and though she knew that wanting and needing were not love, if they were all he could offer her, she would grasp them with both hands, giving him the love of her heart and soul as well as her body, in the hope that one day he would come to love her too.

'But it's I who've got to go to him,

for I know he'll never come to me.'

The weekend with her parents dragged. Though she had made her decision and was determined to phone Nicholas, she wanted to wait until she was alone in her flat. She had no clue as to what his reaction would be, but she wanted no one with her when she found out; and so she knew there was no question of telephoning from under her mother's eagle eye. She did consider writing him a letter, but decided against that idea. She wanted to hear his response to her call and anyway a letter might go astray and if he chose not to reply she would never be sure whether he had received it or not. No, she must phone, and the call must wait until she could make it from home.

⋆ ⋆ ⋆

She arrived back in Grayston-on-Sea late on Bank Holiday Monday evening. As the taxi took her from the station and drove along the promenade, she looked out over the sea. The full moon made a silver pathway across its restless waters, tossing diamonds of spray as it splashed gently on the beach. How different from the ugly grey violence of the winter sea, pounding upon the sea wall, swirling through the streets and carrying all before it.

Thoughts of the storm brought immediate thoughts of Nicholas, and Petra felt the now familiar heartache. It was too late to phone this evening, but at least she only had to wait another twenty-four hours before she could call.

Tuesday crawled by. Tom was back from his two day honeymoon, and talking of the real honeymoon he and Melanie planned as soon as college was closed for the summer vacation. Petra saw students, gave her opening archaeology lecture to her second years, ate nothing and waited for the moment when she could go home and dial Nicholas' number.

When she did reach her flat she made

herself drink a cup of tea before phoning and then taking several deep breaths lifted the receiver. Her hands shook as she dialled and her whole body felt weak and feeble as she waited, listening to the ringing tone. At last it stopped and a woman answered.

'Is that Mrs. Romilly?' asked Petra huskily.

'Yes. Can I help you?'

'I wondered if I could possibly speak with your son?' she said, trying to sound calm.

'I'm awfully sorry,' replied Mrs. Romilly, 'but I'm afraid he's not here.'

'Not there? Oh, well, do you think you could tell me when you expect him back?'

'I'm afraid I don't. He left for Greece this morning and he'll be away for several months, probably till early October.'

'October!' echoed Petra. She had missed him. He had left that morning and she had missed him.

'Can I help?' Mrs. Romilly was asking.

'No, no thank you very much.' Petra's voice trailed away.

'Who is it speaking, please?'

'Just a friend. Petra. Thank you very much.'

Gently, Petra replaced the receiver. If she had phoned last night, when she first got in, she would have caught him. She might not have been able to see him, but at least she could have spoken to him and heard his voice. Now, maddeningly, it was too late. Perhaps it always had been.

9

The summer was wet and tedious, but as before Petra flung herself into her work, knowing she had to keep her mind occupied and herself at exhaustion point so that the time would pass until October when Nicholas would return to England. She still derived pleasure and satisfaction from her job and she was especially pleased with the work done on the archaeology course by the second years. The flame of interest kindled by Nicholas at the conference had grown stronger and it was with pleasure that Petra heard that three of her students were planning to join a dig during the summer vacation.

'You should come with us,' one of them, Diana Hill, said, laughing. 'Keep us in order.'

Petra laughed too. 'I doubt if I could,' she said. 'But you'll have far more fun on your own. Though you do realise, don't you, that if you should find anything you'll be brushed aside and the experts will take over.'

They all laughed then. 'Of course,' said one, Sarah Drayton. 'But we remembered what he said and we want to be part of it.'

'What who said?' asked Petra puzzled.

'Professor Romilly, of course. He said at the lecture that we'd be welcome if we could find our own way there.'

'You're going to Thessos?' Petra was incredulous.

'Of course, didn't we say?'

'No,' said Petra lamely, 'you just said Greece.'

'Well, it's Thessos. If we can get as far as Athens there's an island boat that goes out to Thessos, among other places. We'll take that. Sure you don't want to come?'

This last was said with a grin and Petra managed to return it as she replied, 'Quite sure. I already have plans.'

It was quite untrue, she had nothing

planned and when the college closed for the summer vacation the following week, she had still made none. Tom and Melanie were going to Yugoslavia for two weeks, 'For our real honeymoon,' as Tom put it, and various other members of staff were off to far-flung places. Petra, though restless, could think of nowhere she wanted to go, except Thessos of course, but there was no way she could turn up there uninvited.

Knowing enforced idleness would be the worst possible thing, she spent the first weekend of the holidays with her parents after which she invited herself up to Cumbria to stay with Mary for ten days. But there were still nearly ten weeks before the college year began again and to Petra they stretched into infinity.

* * *

Travelling back from Cumbria, she decided to try and get a part-time job, and got as far as buying a local newspaper at the station to look for something, but when she got back to the flat there was an air letter waiting for her which entirely changed her plans. The stamps were Greek and the address was written in Nicholas' bold hand.

Shaking, she picked it up and carried it through to the living-room. Then she sat down, drew a deep breath and opened it. Inside there was an airline ticket and a single sheet of paper. The ticket was for a return flight to Athens, and on the paper it simply said, '*Please come. Nicholas*.'

Petra stared down at the contents of the envelope. She couldn't believe what she saw. The ticket was dated for July 31st. She glanced at the date on her watch. July 31st was tomorrow. Her immediate reaction was 'I can't possibly go, I've no time to get ready.' But even as she thought this she knew from the crazy leap of joy in her heart that she was going. Somehow she would be on that flight, come hell or high water. She looked at her watch again. She had precisely eighteen hours to organise herself, pack and be at the airport for the flight.

Why he had sent the ticket, what had made him contact her at all, she did not know. Perhaps it was because she had rung his home, and his mother had mentioned it in a letter. Petra neither knew nor cared, but whatever the reason she was determined not to waste this chance; her second and probably last chance to be with Nicholas and her only chance to set the misunderstandings to rights.

With a singing heart she phoned her parents, did some laundry, found her passport and packed her case before she allowed herself a few hours sleep. Next morning she rushed to the bank and then caught the London train. By two o'clock she was in the air and on her way to Nicholas.

She had been so busy, she'd had no time to think once her decision was made, but as the plane droned its way across Europe, doubts began to assail her. What should she do when she arrived? She had no way of contacting him, and hadn't even let him know she was coming. If she hadn't gone to Mary's she might have had the letter days earlier. If she'd stayed in Cumbria any longer she would have missed the opportunity altogether. Her heart skipped a beat at that thought. Would he be at the airport? He knew after all which flight she'd be on, if she were coming.

'Please let him be there,' she prayed. 'Please let him be there, and help me not to waste my second chance.'

As the aeroplane circled Athens, Petra could see the city spread below bathed in the hot afternoon sun. It shimmered faintly in the heat haze and Petra gazed at it sprawling beneath her, hoping and praying Nicholas was down there somewhere waiting for her.

⋆ ⋆ ⋆

The plane landed and taxied in towards the airport buildings. Petra followed the crowd on to the airport bus and then up into the luggage hall.

While she was waiting for her case to appear, she took the opportunity of going into the ladies and renewing her make-up. She gazed into the mirror there, and seeing a pale face staring back at her from huge navy eyes, she wondered how she would look to Nicholas. Quickly she applied more make-up, trying to add a touch of colour to her cheeks; then she brushed her hair and re-coiled it into a knot on the top of her head. It was cooler off her neck, and wearing her hair up always gave her confidence. She had travelled in a cool linen dress, and smoothing the skirt from her hips she gave one last glance in the mirror and went to collect her luggage.

When at last the suitcases came through, Petra found hers easily and made her way out through the customs hall. Nobody stopped her and all at once she was in the general concourse, where a crowd of people awaited the passengers.

She scanned the group quickly and felt herself droop with disappointment. Nicholas wasn't there. Tall as he was, he would have over-topped most of the people around him, clearly visible amongst the rest.

For a moment, Petra paused uncertainly, wondering what to do, and she was just deciding to see if there was a message for her at the airline desk when she saw a face she recognised. Nicholas hadn't come to meet her, but Diana Hill, one of her students, had.

She slid out of the crowd and stepped in front of Petra. 'Hello, Miss Hinton,' she said cheerfully. 'Old Nick says he's sorry he couldn't meet you himself, but it's difficult for him to leave the site.'

A little taken aback at this reception Petra said faintly, 'Old Nick?'

Diana giggled. 'Prof. Romilly. It's what they call him on the site. Very appropriate, actually. He can be a bit of a devil. Workwise I mean. He's an absolute stickler for detail, particularly in the recording and drawing of each layer, but he does take the trouble to explain as well. David Horton, one of the supervisors, says he's one of the best directors there are, so we're very lucky. Shall we go?'

A little bemused at this sudden burst of information, Petra let Diana take her suitcase and followed her out of the airport and into a taxi.

'Piraeus,' Diana directed the driver and they were soon speeding through the outskirts of Athens. 'We weren't sure you'd be on that flight,' said Diana settling back, 'but Old Nick said to wait for the next one from London if you weren't.'

Petra, who was calmer now that the disappointment at finding Diana rather than Nicholas had lessened, said, 'It was very good of you to come all the way just to find me. I could have got to Thessos by myself, you know.'

‘Oh, I know,’ said Diana airily, ‘but I didn’t mind. Actually,’ she confided, ‘I was glad to come. It’s back-breaking work out there in the sun.’

‘You’re very brown,’ said Petra looking at the girl’s healthy suntanned face. ‘You make me feel disgustingly white.’

‘You’ll be brown enough after a few days bending with your trowel all day,’ promised Diana. ‘That is if you’ve come to work on the site.’

‘Of course I have,’ said Petra quickly, wondering what Nicholas had told them.

‘We’re camping just near by,’ said Diana. ‘It’s such a perfect place. Do you know there are no cars on the island? It’s too small. Everyone uses bikes or rides donkeys.’

* * *

They drove along the marina at Piraeus and Diana pointed out the yachts lying alongside the quay and riding at moorings in the bay.

'Gin palaces,' she said, 'for the rich and famous. I'm afraid the boat we take leaves a lot to be desired. It's, well, it's just so Greek. You'll see what I mean.'

She paid off the taxi and led Petra through the confused noise on the dockside to a small vessel making ready to sail. It was much as Petra had imagined, small, dirty and salt-caked, not much more than an old and battered fishing-boat, converted to take passengers. One quick glance into the cramped interior passenger accommodation decided them to settle for a place in the fresh air on deck.

They found an empty corner by the rail at the stern and Petra staked their claim while Diana went in search of chairs. She found none unoccupied, so they simply sat on the deck, their backs against a locker and waited for the boat to sail. The evening sun, still hot and bright, streamed down on to them, and Petra closed her eyes, letting its warmth surround her, sink into her, so that she began to relax even on the uncomfortably hard deck.

'Well, I'm here,' she thought, 'and soon I'll be on Thessos with Nicholas. Why did he ask me to come? Why have I come?' The answer to the second question was easy, but to find the answer to the first she must still wait.

As the boat chugged out of the harbour into the Aegean Sea, Petra and Diana stood at the rail watching the receding shore. A faint breeze ruffled their hair and the sun, slowly slipping towards the horizon in a blaze of red and gold, warmed their faces and tinged their cheeks with pink.

Diana had some food in her bag and they picnicked on the deck before huddling together to doze the night away.

The journey to Thessos took several hours and Petra awoke to find the dawn rising out of the sea, golden, silver and rose against a butter-milk sky. She stood at the rail gazing in wonder at the miraculous colours before her, while the darkness faded behind her.

Diana joined her and suddenly pointing out across the water said, 'There's Thessos.'

Petra screwed her eyes against the brilliance of the morning and saw the dark hump of an island silhouetted against the dawn, an island floating darkly in the gold and silver setting of the sea.

The sky continued to lighten as they stood and watched and from the dark outline emerged the details of the island, no longer in shadow. As Diana had said, Thessos was very small. A fishing village clung to one end, looking for all the world as if it might up-end the land and sink into the sea. Its white sun-baked houses climbed the rocky hillside above the harbour, watching out across the sea for the return of its fishermen.

A jutting harbour wall protected the shore from the winter seas, but now, basking in the hot sunshine, it did no more than divide one smooth patch of water from another. The boat slowed as it neared the harbour and manoeuvred round the protecting wall to lie alongside the quay.

* * *

Petra was surprised at the number of passengers who left the boat, but Diana told her they would almost all be back aboard when it sailed on in about an hour's time.

'They come ashore and visit the street market, and then go on somewhere bigger to stay. Very few people actually stay here, it's quite unspoilt so far. I suppose in time . . .' Her voice trailed off as she looked across the harbour. Then she said briskly, 'Old Nick says there's a tent you can have out at the site or there's a room free in the town if you'd rather.' Diana watched Petra's face as she spoke and added, 'Most of us are out at the site; it's marvellous to sleep out under the stars.'

'I'll take the tent,' said Petra decisively; being away from the site in the town somewhere was not at all in line with her plans.

Diana grinned. 'Right, well let's get out there.'

In the shade of a fig tree in the dusty square beyond the harbour, Diana found a donkey cart and swinging Petra's case into it, had its sleepy driver take them out to the site.

It was a bumpy, twisting ride. The road was little more than a track, hard-baked and dusty and very uneven. It wound away from the village through a large olive grove, where the gnarled and twisted trees fluttered silvery leaves in the sea breeze, and then up the hillside parallel with the shore for a mile before winding down again to a flat plateau, a patchwork of rock and stones, dried grasses and scrubby bushes. At the far end was more sea, smooth and shining blue and between the two were the excavations of the site.

The site itself was fenced off with a single strand of wire slung between posts. Within the fence were some wooden huts — the site offices, Diana told Petra, where the records were made and the artefacts stored. Beyond these the land sloped down to the sea and there were some tall trees and a patch of dusty grass, and the tents of the work force.

'Old Nick'll be in there — ' she added, pointing to the end hut — 'that's his lair. If you need any help with your tent or anything just give a call, Mark and Sarah and I'll be more than pleased to give you a hand.'

Petra stood watching the girl run towards the encampment in the trees for a moment and then turned back to the site. The sky arched, a cloudless blue, above her, as she stared across the excavations. Groups were working carefully in separate places, removing soil with trowels and sifting it into barrows. There were pegs marking out the horizontal levels and plastic tags of different colours labelling the layers.

'I'm glad you came.'

* * *

Nicholas had approached her from behind and the sound of his deep voice made her start. Suddenly shy, 'Nicholas!' was all she could say. She looked up at his face, tanned dark brown by the sun, and smiled unsteadily as her heart turned somersaults.

'Did you have a good trip? Diana found you all right?' Nicholas spoke easily and naturally as he picked up her case. There was no constraint in his manner; no awkwardness at the memories which must have been in his mind, as they were in Petra's.

Petra, determined to match his calm, said, 'Yes, thank you.' She wanted to ask why he'd sent the ticket, to know what had prompted him, but a warning voice inside her cautioned her to wait until the time was right. So she said,

'Isn't this the most glorious place? It's a paradise.'

Nicholas agreed. 'Come on, let's dump your case in the office and I'll show you round.'

He led her round the site, pausing at each group to explain what it was doing. There were trays laid out and marked with coloured labels which corresponded with the layer labels and from several of these Nicholas lifted items and studied them for a moment. There were questions from the supervisor of each group too and this made their progress leisurely.

At last they reached the huts again and Nicholas showed her where the artefacts and other remains were taken from their trays and placed in polythene bags and labelled. In another hut were two women indexing, filing and cross referencing the accumulating information so that should Nicholas need to know anything about any particular area of the work, the information so far collected could be retrieved with ease.

In the last hut, Nicholas introduced Petra to the site supervisor, his second-in-command, and at Petra's request, arranged for her to join with the diggers next day.

'I'll get some of the lads to put up your tent,' Nicholas said when they were outside in the sun once more. 'We all eat together usually. Jane's in charge of the cooking. You could probably help her today if you want to be useful.' He led her off the site and across to the encampment, carrying her case for her.

The camp was arranged like a small tent village, the tents themselves dotted around under the trees and a rough open circle of grass in the middle.

Nicholas left Petra with Jane and with a brief wave of his hand returned to the site.

It was easy to slip into the routine of the camp. Breakfast was always early, to allow them to work several hours before the heat of the day forced them into the shade. The mid-day meal was taken and then most people had a siesta, or swam from the little beach below the camp. Work started again later in the afternoon and finished as twilight stole across the island. If Petra hadn't been so tense, it would have been idyllic.

10

After that first tour of the excavations, Petra didn't see Nicholas alone again. Whenever he was near her, so were several other people, either in the camp or on the site. He didn't exactly avoid her, but he made no effort to detach her from the crowd and so there was no chance of private conversation between them.

Petra worked with her group every day, digging and sifting, or barrowing away the soil. The sun streamed down without respite and she was soon as brown as everyone else, while her hair, always fair, was bleached almost white. It was hard, back-breaking work as promised, but she found it fascinating. Soaked by the sun, and working hard, Petra's appetite increased enormously. When she joined the group for meals she did more than justice to Jane's cooking, and she acquired the same healthy glow she had noticed on Diana at the airport.

She enjoyed being part of the group, but she needed time alone as well. When most of the others were dozing after lunch, she often braved the heat of the afternoon and set off to explore the island, following the narrow tracks worn bare by the numerous goats which wandered the hills searching out the scant pasture. These were herded by the village boys who grinned at her cheekily as she passed, and watching them Petra felt they could have been the same boys who had once inhabited the settlement now being excavated. Time had stood still on Thessos and though the twentieth century had arrived in the form of culture-seeking tourists and bicycles, it was a mere veneer laid on the old way of life.

Nicholas was usually busy in his 'lair' at that time of day, and made no effort to join Petra's explorations. She began to wonder if she would ever see him alone, and several times was tempted to try and speak to him, but she feared a rebuff and continued to hold her peace. The time must come. If it hadn't been for her uncertainty about Nicholas she would have been utterly happy, but at the back of her mind nagged the questions, 'Why did he ask me to come and then ignore me?' and even more, 'Why does he think I came?'

On the following Saturday, Diana called to Petra, 'We're all going into the village this evening. They usually end up dancing in the square. It's great fun. Are you coming?'

'Why not?' answered Petra. 'How do we get there?'

'On bikes,' the girl replied. 'There are several about, I'll get one for you.'

It was an even bumpier journey on a bicycle than it had been in the donkey cart, and extremely hard work pedalling up the hill, but at last they made it and cruised down, laughing, into the village.

It was the hour of the promenade,

and the village was alive with people. The taverna in the square was overflowing and the tables outside were crowded. Petra and her students, all of whom now regarded her as just Petra, had a drink together and then she told them she was going to explore the town.

The tiny shops were still open, and Petra wandered in and out, pushing her way through beaded curtains to their cool dark interiors. There were the usual tourist souvenirs, onyx and carved olive wood, shawls, and embroidered skirts. Petra promised to buy herself one of the shawls before she went home, but for now she was content to drift in and out of the shops without making any purchases.

At last she returned to the square, her eyes searching the crowds for the others. There was music now, fiddles and a zither were being played and some people were dancing already. It was hopeless to spot her own friends, with so many people milling about.

Petra decided to stay put at a table outside the taverna and wait for them to find her.

* * *

As she sipped a cool beer, she was suddenly aware of someone near her, and turning she found Nicholas standing watching her. He came over and said, 'May I join you?'

Petra, used by now to the reaction of her heart when she saw him unexpectedly, said as calmly as she could, 'Yes. Please do.'

He sat down, his smile gleaming white in the dark tan of his face. 'Did you come alone?' he asked.

Petra shook her head. 'No, with Diana, Sarah and Mark. But I explored a bit by myself and I seem to have lost them.'

'Will you come with me for a moment?' said Nicholas suddenly.

'Of course.' Petra felt the excitement building up inside her. Now at last they would be alone and perhaps . . . But she dared not put her hopes into words, even to herself.

Nicholas took her arm and led her away from the square into the warm darkness of the steep and twisting streets beyond. Firmly he held her as he guided her between the houses, winding their way up the hillside. Indeed some of the streets were so steep they turned into flights of broad, shallow steps. There was very little light, for most of the windows of the houses were shuttered and the moon hadn't yet risen. Suddenly they emerged from an alley and Petra found herself clear of the houses, high above the village, with just one large white house in front of them, surrounded by a thick stone wall.

The village was spread below them, its white houses gleaming faintly in the darkness, pinpricks of light dotted about like yellow stars. Far beyond was the glimmer of the sea, where the moon crept over the horizon.

A painted door was set in the garden

wall beside them and Nicholas lifted the latch.

'In here,' he said and pushed the gate wide for Petra to enter. She stepped through and found herself in a quiet walled garden. A lantern hanging from the corner of the house beside it gave a dull yellow glow. Somewhere there was the splashing of water, a fountain perhaps, and everywhere was the heavy fragrance of the flowers, jasmine, bougainvillaea and many Petra couldn't recognise, overflowing from their tubs and flower beds and climbing the walls of the house.

'What a perfect place,' said Petra softly as the quiet embraced her. Far away she could hear the music from the square, but it belonged to a different world. Time stood still in this garden, it was apart from the world, secluded and still.

'It belongs to a friend of mine,' replied Nicholas. 'I often come here when I need to be alone.' He led her to a seat beneath a twisted fig tree and they sat together allowing the peace to wash over them, enfold them and cut them off from the world.

* * *

'It must be now,' Petra thought. 'This is the moment we've both been waiting for.' But she didn't speak, for her heart was so full that she couldn't begin. Instead she looked up at him, his face shadowed in the half-light of the lantern and found herself trembling at the expression she saw in his eyes.

Nicholas had little use for words either and with one hoarse whisper of 'Petra!' he gathered her into his arms, turning her so she was cradled against him, and began to kiss her, his mouth fierce and demanding as it took hers. As before Petra felt her own passion rising to match his as he strained her to him, her breasts crushed against his chest, the fingers of one hand tangled in her hair, those of the other pressing her body to his.

Returning kiss for kiss she clung to him, afraid that this reality might turn out to be another of the dreams of him which haunted her.

At last he raised his head, and while still holding her close looked deep into her eyes. Suddenly shy at what he might see there, Petra turned her head and buried her face in his chest.

'Now then, young lady,' he said firmly, 'you've some explaining to do.'

She tried to sit up and Nicholas allowed her to do so while still keeping a firm hold on her hands as if he feared she might escape him.

'You told me you were going to marry Tom Davies.'

'Tom married someone else,' replied Petra in a small voice.

Nicholas said gently, 'Poor darling, did you mind very much?'

'I didn't mind at all,' said Petra quietly. 'I was never going to marry Tom.'

'What?' cried Nicholas. 'But you said . . . You told me . . . '

'I know what I told you, Nicholas, and I'm truly sorry, but there was a reason.'

'What reason?'

'The best reason, or so I thought at the time,' said Petra. 'Tom said . . . ' she paused awkwardly.

'Tom said?' Nicholas prompted.

'Tom said you were married and I couldn't face being just your mistress.'

'I see.' Nicholas' voice was harsh but it softened as he went on, 'I'm not married, Petra. I was, but my wife, Anne, was killed in a car crash.'

'I know,' wailed Petra. 'I know that now, but I didn't then.' She turned away from him and fought down her tears before she said, 'I was so happy when we were together that night in the flat, and then the next day Tom said — '

'Tom said!' interrupted Nicholas angrily. 'Damn what Tom said. What about me? Why didn't you ask me, for heaven's sake?'

'I tried to find out by myself. I didn't just accept his word,' said Petra defensively. 'I'd been wrong about you before, and this time I wanted to be certain, make sure of my facts before I spoke to you.'

'Well,' said Nicholas, 'you seem to have got them wrong again even so. What did you do to find out?'

'I read the blurb on your books, I looked you up in *Who's Who*. All of them said you were married, so I rang your home. A woman answered and said she was Mrs. Romilly, Mrs. Anne Romilly.'

'My mother,' said Nicholas gently. 'Well, stepmother. Her name is Anne as well.'

'I didn't know it was. I assumed it was — was your Anne. And somehow I couldn't face you with that.' Petra sighed wearily. 'That's why I told you I was going to marry Tom. I hoped that if I didn't see you again, I'd forget you.' At this the tears she had been trying to hold back began to trickle down her cheeks and she turned her face away again so he shouldn't see them.

‘Did you?’ It was almost a whisper as if he were holding his breath for the answer. ‘Did you forget me?’

‘No.’

‘Do you still want to?’

‘No.’ Her voice came out on a sob and it was too much for Nicholas’ self-control. He pulled her into his arms once more and rocked her gently like a baby, until her sobs died away and she lay still against him.

Plucking up courage at last she said, ‘What made you send me the ticket? Why did you ask me to come out here?’

‘Because I wanted you. When I heard from your students that you hadn’t married Tom at all, and that he’d in fact married someone else, it gave *me* hope,’ explained Nicholas. ‘You see, I’d tried to forget you too. But I couldn’t do it either. You haunted me. I loved you too much.’

‘Does anyone else come into this garden?’ asked Petra suddenly.

Nicholas was surprised at the sudden change of subject. ‘No, I don’t think so, not often anyway. Why?'

'Please, will you kiss me again?' She looked up at him and he caught the sparkle of her eyes in the lantern light. For a long moment his gaze held hers and then he said, 'You know what'll happen if I do!'

Petra put up a hand to his cheek and said softly, 'Yes, I know. That's why I asked you.'

'Witch!' groaned Nicholas, and putting her from him he got to his feet. Then he took her hand and led her to a door in the side of the house.

'Where are we going?' she asked, surprised.

'I keep a room here, too. We'll have more privacy there, and I want you to myself.'

* * *

They went into the cool and silent house and he led her up a narrow stair to a room overlooking the garden they had just left. The heady fragrance of the white jasmine which grew outside the window filled the air and the room was faintly-lit by moon glow from over the sea. Gently Nicholas closed the door behind them, and Petra turned to him, but he placed his hands on her shoulders, holding her away, looking into her questioning face.

'We've come a long way from that January day in the basement flat,' he said lifting one hand to twist a strand of her hair loosely round his fingers. 'I'll never forget how you looked then, in a towering rage, quite beautiful, even as you hurled abuse at me.'

'Don't remind me,' begged Petra. 'I'm still so ashamed of myself when I think about that.'

'Don't be,' said Nicholas. 'You were the first woman who had made me aware of her, since Anne died.' He paused and captured Petra's hands in his, holding them firmly as he went on, 'All my happiness seemed to die with Anne,' he said, 'but you brought me to life again. When I kissed you that first time I felt disloyal to Anne's memory. That was silly, she would never have wanted me to live my life alone; or begrudged me a second chance of happiness, but I'd always been so sure I couldn't love anyone else. And yet, with you, I couldn't help myself. I couldn't bear not to hold you in my arms. I loved Anne, she was, and is, part of my life, part of me, but I love you, Petra, I love you because you're you, and I can't live the rest of my life without you. Do you understand what I'm trying to say?'

Petra heard the uncertainty in his voice and she felt a wave of love surge through her. Gently she drew him to her and kissed him before she said, 'Oh, Nicholas Romilly, don't ever leave me again. Without you I'm nothing.'

'Love me?' he asked, a hopeful twinkle in his eye.

Petra gave an enchanted giggle. 'Well,' she said, considering, darting a look at him from under her lashes.

'Well?' said Nicholas dangerously, his fingers tightening on her arms.

'Sometimes I love you so much it hurts,' she admitted, 'and sometimes I love you more. Nicholas!' she cried out his name as he gathered her up and tossed her on to the little bed which stood beneath the window.

'That does it,' he said, dropping down beside her. 'You're stuck with me for life.'

'Promise?' she murmured, reaching up for him.

'Oh yes, angel,' he breathed. 'I promise.'

THE END

We do hope that you have enjoyed reading this large print book.

Did you know that all of our titles are available for purchase?

We publish a wide range of high quality large print books including:
Romances, Mysteries, Classics
General Fiction
Non Fiction and Westerns

Special interest titles available in large print are:
The Little Oxford Dictionary
Music Book, Song Book
Hymn Book, Service Book

Also available from us courtesy of Oxford University Press:
Young Readers' Dictionary
(large print edition)
Young Readers' Thesaurus
(large print edition)

For further information or a free brochure, please contact us at:
Ulverscroft Large Print Books Ltd.,
The Green, Bradgate Road, Anstey,
Leicester, LE7 7FU, England.
Tel: (00 44) **0116 236 4325**
Fax: (00 44) **0116 234 0205**

Other titles in the
Linford Romance Library:

TOO CLOSE FOR COMFORT

Chrissie Loveday

Emily has shut herself away to work in the family's old holiday cottage in remotest West Cornwall. Her two Jack Russells are all the company she needs . . . until the night she rescues a stranger injured in a raging storm. Cut off by bad weather, and with no telephone, they have to sit it out. Emily begins to warm to Adam. But who is he — and why does he want to stay with her once the storm has passed?

CHRISTMAS CHARADE

Kay Gregory

When Nina Petrov meets charismatic businessman Fenton Hardwick on a transcontinental train to Chicago, she sees him as the solution to her recurring Christmas problem. Every year her matchmaking father produces a different hopelessly unsuitable man for her to marry. Nina decides she needs a temporary fiancé to get him off her case, and Fen seems the perfect candidate for the job — until she makes the mistake of trying to pay him for his help . . .

A LETTER TO MY LOVE

Toni Anders

Devastated when Marcus married someone else, Sorrel resolved to devote her life to her toyshop and her invalid cousin, Alyse. However, when she meets Carl, the Bavarian woodcarver, it provides a romantic distraction — but Marcus's growing friendship with Alyse unsettles Sorrel. She is torn between her still-present love for Marcus, and her cousin's happiness. When Marcus's spiteful sister, Pamela, decides to repossess the toyshop for a wine bar, Sorrel decides to fight them both.

DOCTOR, DOCTOR

Chrissie Loveday

The arrival of a new doctor in a small Cornish hospital causes a stir, especially among the female members of staff. Lauren has worked hard to build her career, along with a protective shell to keep her emotions intact. She won't risk being hurt again, but Tom has other ideas . . . As they share the highs and lows of hospital life, they develop a mutual respect for each other's professional skills — but can there ever be more to their relationship?

YOURS FOR ETERNITY

Janet Whitehead

Danielle McMasters was haunted by the memory of the man she had loved and lost in a fatal car crash six years before. Ben was dead. So who, then, was the man watching her from across the room? His likeness was uncanny — it had to be Ben . . . hadn't it? But how could he have returned from the grave — and why was someone following her every move? The past was haunting her present, but how would it affect her future?